"Is this the right way to treat highly skilled professionals from India? What an eye – opener" – Anonymous.

"A light hearted fiction which makes you think" – Fellow Author.

"Writing style relates to Youth and Adult" – Anonymous.

"A perfect coming of age story, quite relatable to a lot of students"- Fellow Author.

Thank you, Dad Mom, Wifey and Ayaan for making my book dreams come alive!

ONFUSED……….5

PRAYER……….16

IS COMING TO AN END……30

ι……….38

B VISA……….49

CHAPTER 6 - DOLLAR, DOLLAR, DOLLAR……….59

CHAPTER 7- REUNION……….72

CHAPTER 8 - NEW AGE SLAVERY……….84

CHAPTER 9 - PACK OF CARDS……….97

CHAPTER 10 - MARKET COMES CRASHING DOWN….111

CHAPTER 11- BREAKING EVEN……….128

CHAPTER 12- ROCK BOTTOM……….143

CHAPTER 14 - VICTORY AT LAST……….156

CHAPTER 1 - LOST AND CONFUSED

Amit was dizzy, he had not felt like this ever before. He was falling fast through space, the wind whipping in his face and the flap of his shirt slapping his ears. Through all this he wasn't the least bit scared, maybe it was the burst of color all around him assaulting his senses. He tried to reach out to touch the color wall, but his hand went right through it. For someone falling through thin air to an unknown fate he was strangely calm, like he felt expectant for whatever fate he might meet. Suddenly, he felt a hand pull him up from this free fall and right out of his bright surroundings. His eyes opened then to take in his new surroundings. He was on his bed and his mother still had him by the forearm trying to wake him from his slumber. Her face was wreathed in smiles as she shook him awake roughly, calling out his name loudly.

"Wake up *Beta*, you might miss your flight."

In a flash, everything came back to Amit. He jumped up from the bed, the excitement jolting through him. He was going to America today. He would finally see the land of opportunities!

"Good morning mom!" he greeted excitedly, clasping his hands together in front of his face.

"Good morning son," his mother smiled at him as he bounded to the bath house to get ready for the next phase of his life.

In the car with his dad, mom, granny and his younger sister Pooja on the way to the airport, Amit stared out through the window watching the streets and sights of Mumbai rush past him in a semi blur. It was reminiscent of his dream earlier this morning, somehow the color represented his life and everything beautiful in it and the free fall represented his uncertain future. Somehow the feeling of excitement stayed with him through it all. He was not scared of what he would find in DC, he was after all going to find a better future and the uncertainty did nothing to quell his good spirits.

They got to Mumbai airport and Amit had to endure his mom and granny's smoldering and pieces of advice that was given time and time again.

"Remember to call when you touch down," mom said, tears shining in her eyes.

"Don't forget to write us about your school and everything you find exciting," granny said into his face as she held him affectionately on both sides of his face."

"Pranam Amma," he clasped his hands in greeting to her after he had touched her feet, hoping it was goodbye finally.

"Don't forget to eat well and sleep well," mom quipped in too not quite finished. His father stood a little way from them smiling with his hands folded across his chest. He was looking at the women with an accommodating gaze as if enjoying the antics of a petulant child. Amit knew he cared too but he would not show it. It wasn't 'manly' to show emotion in front of women his father had told him on several occasions. But Amit would really appreciate it if his father would break up this little farewell party that was soon turning into a crying jag between the two women.

It was Pooja instead who came to his rescue in her cheery manner. "He's not leaving forever mom! Why treat him like he is going to die there?" Amit's mom glared at Pooja through her tear stained face and took a swat at her as she skipped away laughing. Amit cast a grateful look her way from saving him from the embarrassing situation.

They took him to his departure gate and said their goodbyes. Amit endured the hugs and kisses once more and hugged his father, who tapped him on the back; his universal sign of pride and approval. He touched his feet too and whispered; "Pranaam" to him too in a tear choked voice. His father had been his hero growing up. He was only taking this direction in his life because he hoped he would be a better computer programmer than his father and make him very proud of him. Amit hugged Pooja, ruffling her neatly parked hair with a mischievous smile on his face. "Take care of yourself Pooj." he whispered in her ears as she struggled to get out of his embrace, a mock frown on her face.

He walked away from them towards the boarding area, hoping he made all these people who loved him proud.

****

Dulles International airport was very different from Mumbai airport. That was the first thought that registered in Amit's mind when he alighted from the plane. It had been a very long and tiring flight, but the almost electric energy that charged his environments cured him of his lethargy fast.

The sights and the sounds of his new environment were incredible. As he passed one of the many food court areas in the airport, his nose took in the delicious smells, including cinnamon buns, pizza and even hot dogs and sauerkraut. He was amazed at the crowd of people who seemed oblivious to each other as they made their way towards their destinations. In front of him were a group of business executives, wearing suits that cost more money than Amit had ever seen in his lifetime. They were all talking on their cell phones or using their Blackberry devices, no doubt making deals that would eventually make them richer. Amit secretly vowed that one day soon he would wear such fine suits and carry the latest high-tech devices with him. Of course, he would have to have someone teach him how to use those gadgets, but he would cross that bridge when he came to it.

This was quite different from the chaos he had left behind in the Mumbai airport. There people were rowdy, and greetings were hurled across the space not caring who listened. Some people were escorted to the airport with an entourage of relatives and well-wishers and Amit was very glad he was spared that treatment.

Amit finally arrived at the immigration and customs checkpoint with the cluster of thoughts and questions irking his mind. *Would they stop me from entering the country if I don't have the right documents? Would they expect me to answer questions in American accent? Would they ask me about money or the mango achaar' I am carrying in my black bag?* Those and a few dozen other questions raced through his mind, and he felt his palms getting sweaty. He would have to remember to wipe his hands across his trousers before meeting with airport officials; he certainly did not want to be pulled out of line and branded as a terrorist simply because he was nervous and excited at the same time.

His bladder suddenly needed relief and he started searching frantically for the restroom. He finally saw the restroom sign at the end of the hall, but he could not muster up the courage to step out of the line. This reminded him of the almost panic attack he had had at the US consulate during his interview, he had been so strung tight after standing in a queue from 3:30 a.m. in the morning. The Hispanic lady behind him had started looking at him funny and he couldn't blame her, his movements had become jerky and his armpits were drenched. Even in his anxiety, he found her mistrustful gaze funny. How could she be looking at him expecting him to fit a stereotype that was a one size fits all for all people of color?

Finally, it was his turn, the officer was a tall and hefty black American with a body like a body builder. He reminded Amit of bouncers he saw on the television in swanky clubs. The man seemed to give Amit a once over and dismiss him with a snort. Like he had concluded there was nothing to be seen about a skinny and very nervously excited young Indian boy. "So what countries have you visited before coming to the United States?"

Afraid he was going to stumble over his words, he immediately replied; "Sir, Nepal when I was in sixth grade and Dubai in the year 1999." The officer gave him a begrudging nod as if he was surprised this skinny boy had ever been anywhere else but in the backwaters of India. He asked him some other questions with the same perma-frown and strangely, those questions put Amit at ease and made his answers confident and engaging. Amit began thinking he had misjudged this man. Probably the frown was a permanent crease he had on his forehead and he was not really mean. After a few more questions, the officer whose name tag read 'Briggs. D' sent him to baggage claim and then customs office. Amit let out a shuddering breath of relief, he was almost done! The boy from nondescript Virar had now ended up in Washington D.C.

As he stood next to the conveyor belt to collect his baggage, he looked around but couldn't find his green suitcase, the one he had packed his favorite T shirts and CDs. Then he saw something that stopped him cold; he saw a K9 dog sniffing his other bag and trying to almost tear it apart. Somehow the mithai or the Parle- G biscuits his granny had given him which were in the luggage were really opening all the senses of this highly trained, drug sniffing animal. Immediately the dog lady from Customs asked him coolly, leveling her gaze at him; "Do you know what you have in this luggage?"

Amit thought he would fall through the floor, but knew he had to maintain his composure as he answered; "Madam, I think I have some Indian sweets and some bishkit." As if he was unsure he still had the offending items in his possession or it was something else more incriminating.

The Customs lady raised a quizzical brow at me and paused mid action; "Excuse me?"

This time he gestured the action of eating a biscuit and saying *biscuit* and *sweets.* The Customs lady asked him to get to the customs department to take the baggage to the X-ray screening. Amit had heard stories of people paying fines for their pickles and Pappadums. He was told by other people that it would be better to convince the customs lady rather than letting his baggage go to the X ray screening. He almost broke down and told the lady about the lost baggage to gain sympathy from her, but that was no good. Finally, after pleading for a while, he was able to get his luggage without paying any fines. They also helped him find his other missing luggage.

Just then, his bladder reminded him he had not answered nature's call yet and he rushed towards the restroom sign he had seen earlier. He rushed into the shiny toilet stall, the smell of bleach strong and unfamiliar it almost made his eyes tear up. He was taking care of business when he remembered that he had left his luggage outside the toilet beside the door. It was easy target for anyone who wanted to rob him. He had been told stories of people who had been robbed for being careless with their luggage in airports. He hurried up and left, the thought of losing his limited possessions once again driving him to panic. He heaved a sigh of relief as he came out to see his things safe and untampered with. He went through the locks quickly making sure they were intact. He walked towards the exit then, hoping to find a means of transportation, or at least other students going to GW University.

He found a group of boys standing by the tarmac, wearing UW T shirts. They were laughing and horsing around, and they looked like they were waiting for someone. He studied them carefully, hoping there was someone there he could approach, shy as he was. They were mixed race, the tallest guy had blond hair and movie star good looks. He looked like he was mixed race, but he had Caucasian mixed in there, it was dominant. The two other guys looked Chinese, their porcelain skin and squinty eyes gave them away, but they didn't have that unsure almost anxious look around them that screamed new immigrant. So, they definitely had been here their entire time. The last guy was Indian, he was somehow removed from the group even though he joined in their jokes and laughed with them like he was more comfortable in his own company.

Amit approached them, fastening his steps so he wouldn't seem timid. First impressions they say, was everything. "Excuse me," he said cautiously. "Are you also waiting for a shuttle to UW?"

The blond guy sized him up with a quizzical look, but it was the Indian guy who came forward with a smile and attempted to be friendly. "I'm Manoj," he said to him smiling and extending his hands for a handshake. "We are all waiting for a taxi to take us up to UW. Are you newbie too?" his eyes were kind Amit noticed, and he exuded the calm confidence of someone who was comfortable in his own skin. His charisma belied the shy aloofness you saw from afar and Amit found that something to greatly respect.

"Yes, I just arrived."

"You're welcome old boy," the blond guy said a little too fast, the words rolling off his tongue in a strange way. Like they were balls bouncing around in a drum before finally deciding to be flushed out. The words fell from the tip of his lips with a throaty, scratchy quality that Amit would learn later was a Texan accent. "Cheng here is new too from Seoul," he said gesturing to one of the Korean guys who nodded. He seemed like the default second in command of the group who took his directives from Manoj. "I am Brian" he hit Amit on the left shoulder in a show of unwarranted sportsmanship which made Amit jump and elicited a laugh from all of them. The other Korean guy introduced himself as Min Ho and they were still trying to get familiarized when a weird looking Sardarji stopped in front of them.

"Where you go?" he asked them in very broken English. They gave him their address and piled into the yellow taxi.

When they got to the residence hall, Manoj acted the perfect guide and helped Cheng find and settle into his room. After finding out Amit had not made any accommodation plans, Manoj, Brian and Min Ho offered to share their apartment with him for a very affordable price. Amit was very grateful for this as it had reduced his worries by a third. The apartment was a three-bedroom bungalow a few streets away from school. The streets were lined with identical bungalows that with the same color scheme, the only way to differentiate the houses were its numbers and features imperceptible to the eyes of a stranger. It was the fact that some had a chip of paint scraped off the awning or that its shade of red had dulled in some places. Amit was offered the study which had been converted into a room for him, while the other three had taken the three rooms on the ground floor.

The George Washington University (GW, GWU, or George Washington) was a private research university in Washington, D.C. Charted by an act of the United States Congress in 1821, GW was founded on the basis of the wishes of George Washington, 1st President of the United States, for a national university within the nation's capital.

George Washington, the 1st President of the United States, advocated the establishment of a national university in the U.S. capital in his first State of the Union address in 1790 and continued to promote this idea throughout his career and until his death. In his will, Washington left shares in the Potomac Company to endow the university. However, due to the company's financial difficulties, funds were raised independently. On 9 February 1821, the university was founded by an Act of Congress, making it one of only 5 universities in the United States with a Congressional charter.

Now he had to register his courses, get a social security number and find a part time job, Amit checked off these tasks in his head. Top on his priority list was getting a job that could help pay the bills and look good on his CV. After his very tiring and exciting day, Amit was ready to turn in for the night.

Finding a job Amit realized was not as easy as he had envisaged it to be. It had been two weeks in which Amit had registered all his courses and gone through the orientation week. Now classes were to start in earnest, the school rousing from it's almost slumber of the summer vacation like a dragon waking up from a very long nap. Amit had scoured all the small businesses around G-DUB who needed the services of a programmer, computer analyst, web developer or assistant but every position had been filled or they could not afford to take on another staff on their payroll. Apparently, most of these vacancies were filled before school resumed and they had some students who applied by the end of the previous semester and it was done on a first come first serve basis. He came home every night tired out from school and job hunting but he never lost his enthusiasm. Maybe he did it, so his family would not be worried that he was not his upbeat optimistic self whenever they called Amit mused to himself.

The third week though, something gave. Brian came back from classes announcing that Ms. Sophia, one of their lecturers lost her media assistant. She had actually fired him for his clumsiness and tardiness. He advised Amit to apply for the position which he did and luckily, he was given the position. His job was cut and dry; he oversaw the classroom media and he had to operate the VCR, TV and overhead projectors. He also had to move those equipment from class to class and set it up before the lectures started. It was not Amit's ideal job, but at this point he could not afford to be choosy and it would help pay the bills at least.

To celebrate his employment and settling in, his housemates wanted to give him a hazing ceremony of sorts, like a coming of age welcome ceremony. Manoj suggested a strip club, and after much hesitation from Amit and persuasions from Brian-who found every little opportunity to party- they agreed and left. The club was full, one could her the din beneath the loud rock music playing. The speakers seemed to shake the foundation of the building and their neon sign, shining yellow, pink and brown announced a welcome to anyone walking by. It was manned by mean looking bouncers, one of them a black guy who looked to be six feet five and muscles that seemed to stretch his clothes to tearing. But that was not his most intimidating feature; he had a scar that ran through the left half of his face that made him look like a cross between Captain Hook and Blade. When he asked for Amit's ID, he stumbled over himself to get it out and present it to him.

The dancers were already on the stage in all their naked glory, one of them straddling the pole while the other did a strip tease. Everyone was going crazy over their performance, the bolder ones going onstage to put dollar bills in their shoes and between their ass cheeks; that brought a roar of laughter from the audience and a mock frown from the dancer. With a round of applause, they strutted off the stage. The next dancer to come onstage was a nun or was dressed as one Amit reminded himself. He was still caught up by his conservative upbringing, he had thought seeing girls naked would not be such a shock to him since he was far from home and all the restrictions of his culture but that didn't seem to be the case. Apparently, you could take the boy out of India, but you could not take the India out of him. The girl on stage started dancing, moving her nubile body sensually as she undressed, and showing bit by tempting bit of pale flesh in a show of eroticism.

When she took off her top, Amit's breath caught in his throat. He knew her, he would recognize that face anywhere even in the shadow of a strip club and under all that make-up. It was Lisa, they had a class together; computer programming. He had noticed her first day of classes, fresh faced and always ready with a smile. She had effortlessly become Professor Austen's favorite with her intelligent questions and even more so intelligent answers. This had earned her the title of suck up, there wasn't anyone in programming who hadn't heard of Lisa. Amit had become quite smitten by her, drawn by her smiles, beauty and her smartness. He knew that she was way out of his league and it would never work out for them. The question burning through his head then was 'why was she here'?! He had heard of stories of girls who sold themselves for money in college, but it had always been a hypothetical myth to him till now. As she stripped further, Amit tried to control his body's reaction and had little success, he did not want to think of Lisa like that. He was convinced he was in love, if love was the burning feeling he felt in his chest every time other men cheered as she took off pieces of clothing. She was a great dancer Amit acknowledged the fact as she rocked the pole, letting it touch her flesh in very intimate places.

He stifled a surge of jealousy as MinHo and Brian got up to plant dollar bills in her sheer lace panties that left very little to the imagination. He wondered now how he would see her from now on; would he always imagine her naked every time she answered one of Ms. Austen's technical questions. He tried to put her off his mind as his friends had noticed his strange mood, how would he talk about watching his crush dancing when she didn't even know he existed? You couldn't be more pathetic than that. He ordered more drinks instead, testing everything that was on offer as his friends urged to be adventurous and spontaneous in his choices. Soon Lisa was a distant memory wrapped in cotton and cocooned in a very safe part of his brain.

CHAPTER 2- LIVING ON A PRAYER

Everything his friends, the internet and books had said about hangovers did not prepare Amit for the horrible way he felt the next day. He didn't feel like he had a hangover, more like he was death warmed over. His head felt like a million soldiers were stomping through it with spiked boots that embedded itself into his grey matter with every stomp and they all also had ten-ton hammers with which they tortured the tender tissues of his brain. He turned his head gingerly away from the sliver of light coming through the blinds of his converted bedroom. The creaks of the old wooden bed Manoj had given him were no help at all; each creak was a deafening clap in his ears. He sat up and a violent wave of nausea swept through his body, his brain sloshing like murk behind his skull. *I am going to die* he thought to himself pitifully as he struggled to his feet, staggering out of his room and down the stairs to the living room. If he was going to die Amit reasoned, it was better he did so where he would be easily found. He stumbled into the sitting room to find Min Ho downing an awful smelling greenish liquid. He squeezed his face as if in torture and if not for the headache Amit was sporting, it would have made him laugh.

Min Ho looked up as he stumbled in, his eyes as bloodshot as Amit's and he left for the kitchen without a word. Amit lowered himself gingerly onto the long sofa careful not to start up the violent sloshing in his head again. Min Ho reappeared a few minutes later with a cup of the foul-smelling brew again and offered it to Amit wordlessly. Amit stared at it skeptically, not sure he wanted to die by poisoning. "It will take care of the hangover," Min Ho said in his tiny nasal voice.

"What is this?"

"Aloe vera, ginger, honey and salt, the honey is for sweetening," Min Ho explained a little amused at Amit's greenness. Amit took the liquid from him, reasoning that if he was being poisoned, at least it would not be just him going to the great beyond. The taste was as horrible as he had feared; it was choking and coated his tongue like a thick layer of grease that was bitter. He coughed and choked as he swallowed, his throat muscles protesting the murk that it was granting entrance.

"Did you say honey?" Amit asked incredulously as he tried to scrub the awful taste off his tongue. Min Ho laughed then, his eyes lighting up with mirth.

"Whatever you say Amit, I'm off to work."

Work! Amit sat up bolt upright. In the midst of his agony, he had forgotten he had a job to go to and classes right after. He checked the clock; 9:45 am. He squeezed his eyes shut and swore. He was very late! How would he explain to his mom that he had lost his hard-won job in the very first week because he had a hangover from alcohol? His slowly receding headache momentarily forgotten, he bounded up the stairs to get ready ignoring Min Ho's questioning stare. He bounded out of the house swearing to Lord Shiva, Vishnu and Brahma that he would never touch another bottle of alcohol in his life again.

In his hurry to get to the store where the media equipment was for Ms. Sophia's class, he bumped into someone sending their books, stationery and a sheaf of papers flying. He immediately got on his knees helping gather everything he had bumped into while uttering a litany of 'sorrys' that did nothing to preserve some of the paper that was already ruined. People walked by, watching them with mild curiosity as if their misfortune was a passing interest. The girl Amit had bumped into released a torrent of curses as she tried to save her papers from further damage. Amit stopped and looked up at her and his mouth went dry. It was Lisa and before he could help it, the images of her naked sensual body as it moved synchronously on the pole came unbidden to his mind. He blinked wordlessly, stammering his apologies while trying to avoid her gaze.

"Don't I know you from somewhere?" Lisa asked that annoyed frown still on her face. It was as if she were interrogating a petulant child.

"Uuhhm…. I'm…" Amit stumbled over himself finding it difficult to answer her question. Just as he opened his mouth to speak again, he heard Ms. Sophia's voice from behind; "You're late Amit" he turned in a flash to answer her, but she had already walked past him. If he thought this day could not possibly get worse before now, he was wrong. He mumbled more apologies Lisa and sprinted off, praying he could somehow set up the equipment before Ms. Sophia got into class.

He had heard about Ms. Sophia's unbending rules and legendary temper, had also heard about the fate of every intern, research or media assistant -working with her- who had been less than satisfactory. The first time she had spoken to him after he had been hired by her research assistant –Ravi- she had made a point of reminding him of those other people and to intimidate him with her beady eyes. She was an African-American woman with a height and voice meant for intimidation. These features however did not detract from her beauty; full lips on a heart shaped face with a body blessed by the Gods. She probably affected that hard ass persona, so she could be taken seriously in her career. Whatever was the reason for her disposition, it would take a really big miracle for him not to lose his job today. Amit mused as he set up the instruments while Ms. Sophia stood at the end of the class. Her stance was rigid and face tight in annoyance. The negative energy she was giving off was palpable and spread across the class. The students were now giving him sympathetic glances as he tried his best to be fast.

After the end of that class, Amit packed up the equipment and waited in Ms. Sophia's outer office for her to come out and dismiss him. Ravi, her research assistant also sat in the outer office, his eyes recriminating as he stared at Amit. He seemed to enjoy Amit's discomfort and he went on to gloat about how principled he was that he would never be so irresponsible as to treat an important position as this with such contempt.

"Serving Ms. Sophia is an honor I would never dream of spiting," Amit ignored the royal suck up, he had more pressing things to worry about. No wonder Ravi was the longest serving research assistant Ms. Sophia had kept. Just then she came out of her office with the dean of education who had come visiting and after saying their goodbyes, she turned to him.

"Mr. Amit Khanna, this is your first week working with me, yes?" she asked. Amit nodded slowly, knowing what would come and dreading it. "You're new to the school too, yes?" she continued as if she was checking out items in her head.

"Yes, ma'am," she seemed to consider his answers as if to see if they were vital to whatever conversation she was having in her head. They must have, because her next words were totally unexpected.

"Do not be late again, I'll let you off with a warning this time." Amit stared at her open mouthed as she turned on her heels and walked into her inner office. Ravi made a strangled sound of surprise in his throat, staring at Amit as if he had sprouted horns. Amit didn't spare him a glance and walked out before she changed her mind about pardoning him. He didn't care what luck, God or providence had come to his rescue, and he only knew he was the first employee of Ms. Sophia who had not been fired because of tardiness.

That evening, after his classes Amit went to the Gelman library to study a little before he retired for the day. GW University had so many different libraries that it left Amit in awe, every discipline had libraries for further studies and research. Amit had never seen so much space filled with books in his life. He had made a point of visiting all the libraries in G-DUB, so he could breathe the same air as those books. Gelman undergraduate library seemed to be his favorite hangout, it had five floors with the studio and learning rooms on the first floor and its second floor consisted of the multipurpose event space, the computer vet, helpdesk and the reading rooms. The reading room at the end of the south hall always had few people there so Amit found it a haven.

He was deeply engrossed in his notes from Advanced Math class he did not notice someone approaching him till they were almost upon him. He heard the click of heels as the owner tapped the floor with the tips of her Louboutins and he looked up into the most beautiful pair of green eyes he had ever seen. He knew too well who those eyes belonged to, but he was unsure about why they were so intently focused on him. May be she had come to reprimand him for being careless and rude earlier today.

"You're the guy from this morning," she said as if it explained some great mystery she had been trying to unravel. He stared at her not sure if he should answer.

"And I remember you now; you're in my computer programming class!" Why did she have to say everything with an exclamation Amit asked himself, what was she always so excited about?

"I'm sorry about this morning, Amit said without tying up his tongue and swallowing it. She waved her hands as if waiving his apologies away. "It's okay, I wasn't looking where I was going either. What are you reading?"

"Professor Salvatore's notes." He said showing her his textbook and notes. What was wrong with him Amit asked himself, could he stop making a fool of himself in front of this girl?

"What's your name? I can't seem to recall it," her mind was like a butterfly; flitting from topic to topic and perching on what caught her fancy momentarily.

"Amit, Amit Khanna."

"Nice to meet you Amit, I'm Lisa Morgan. I work at the reference desk on the second floor here. Do you come here often?"

"Uhmm, yes…"

"Well that's cool Amit, why don't we get together to study sometime?" his hesitation must have shown on his face because she put on her show stopping smile and all her bargaining power. "Come on, it will be fun. And it would be a good way of making it up to me for ruining my research paper this morning." She completed with a sly smile. Amit nodded wordlessly again, having been reduced to a bumbling idiot in the presence of this strange girl. She smiled widely, turned and left then. From that moment, Amit knew he had answered a siren's call and he wasn't sure if he would survive this voyage.

It was the Indian community orientation week. Amit was excited, at least he would get to meet more people of Indian origin and get a little piece of home that would sustain him for a while. The older Indian students in his school always organized this event yearly for the newbies and this was an opportunity to choose the new Indian community student council leaders. They organized talk shows, seminars on several topics that concerned their academics and G-DUB. They invited professors for those talk shows and seminars, and after those events, the main orientation activities started. It seemed as if they organized those seminars as a required chore that had to be done and gotten out of the way before they went into the singing and dancing part. On Wednesday night, they had a sort of hazing ceremony for the male students where they all went naked and danced around the school courtyard in only their boxer shorts and singing their favorite Indian item numbers (raunchy songs from Bollywood movies). Then they swore an oath of sorts which didn't really mean anything because they were all mostly drunk by then. On Friday night it was the dinner night where they all had an opportunity to mingle and fraternize with the girls. People had been rumored to dump their girlfriends at home after dinner night. But the highlight of the week for Amit was the movie reenactment night.

A popular Indian movie would be announced as the theme of the party and everyone picked a character they could be from the movie. The costumes were beautifully done, and the food was out of this World! Every traditional meal was laid out in style and beauty to overwhelm his taste buds. His favorite dessert; kheer (rice pudding) reminded him so much of home and granny's cooking that he made a point of calling home after the ceremony. The lights were reminiscent of Indian temples during Diwali, satin sheets adorned the halls and corridors and they sang folk songs and danced to them during the reenactment night.

It was one night when all social barriers were swept under the carpet and everyone was just in a non-judgmental and fun environment. Some of the Indian professors sat and played cards with the new students. They greeted them the way you greet a peer and shook their hands. This was a very strange practice for Amit as he had never talked to teachers like that. Teachers in India were very authoritarian and hardly available other than the school schedule. Also, they were not very friendly. Even the formidable professor Imran - a professor of Hardware Engineering at GW whom the students had nicknamed Dumbledore because of his death glare and hat which was somehow pointy- attended the events and played cards too, asking the students to call him with his first name. Still nobody even dared. The students just found ways to not have to mention his name or refer directly to him in conversations, so they would not call him using his first name.

This was a good reprieve for Amit and his roomies since he was fighting one battle after another. Initially the struggle was to get good scores in GRE and TOEFL which required a lot of sleepless nights and cramming words like "gregarious and ostentatious" to name a few followed by the rigorous application process. Each application costed close to 150$ (not to mention the exam fees was around 400$ as well). All these expenses for a lower middle-class family earning in rupees was not easy. His father was a Manager at a local manufacturing company and his salary at his peak time was one lakh rupees a month (less than 2000$). It was not easy to raise a family with that salary in a city close to Mumbai. His Dad always bragged to his friends "One day Amit will make 10 times the money I make in one month" Getting an F-1 visa was also a painful process. Students got in the queues starting at 4 AM to make sure that they were called during the 2-hour window as the interview hours were just 9AM – 11 AM. On an average there were 5000+ people standing in the queue. Amit had to borrow money from his Dad to buy train tickets for Mumbai, hotel stay and visa application which was another 100$ or so. All the expenses added up and his Dad was hopeful that one day these expenses will be worth it. That's why he kept borrowing money either from banks or private lenders with the hope that one day his son will take care of these when he starts earning in dollars.

Finally, Amit's patience paid off and the talent show began. It was performances by Indian students and their friends. The song had a familiar tune. It was a song which was played at almost every wedding in India. "Dholi taro, dhol baje......" All the students and teachers put aside their inhibitions and started dancing and singing in symphony. This was the moment which completely restored Amit's confidence and he was ready to immerse himself in studies and the land of opportunities. The week ended with the election of the new leaders of the student council and Manoj emerged as Indian community student council President. Amit could not say he was particularly surprised; Manoj had always been the default leader in any association he belonged to. With his impeccable qualities, responsibility and aura of confidence. Amit was happy for him and strived to be looked upon and respected as Manoj had become in G-DUB.

****
****

By the end of the semester, Amit had changed a lot; his walk was a lot more confident and every course he aced gave him a bounce to his steps. His study sessions with Lisa had blossomed into a friendship he cherished, he would not dream of ruining what they had because of his feelings for her. They had made each other better, and Lisa had helped him be more confident in oral quizzes. They were a great pair and he ignored his friend's teasing that he had the most sought-after girl on campus at his side and he still would not act. He was tired of telling them they were just friends. Lisa seemed immune to all the snide remarks and teasing. She and her friends had accepted Amit as a fixture in their circle; going on weekend getaways and studying with them. One thing hung over Amit's head like cloud though; it was what he had seen that night at the strip club. He had never gone to that bar again for fear of running into her there and he was grateful his roommates didn't remember Lisa from that night. He had tried to work up the courage to ask her about that part of her life, but his heart always failed him. He hoped she would trust him enough one day to tell him about that side of her.

One incident however, almost broached that subject for them. They had been studying the calculus open quiz for their advanced calculus class in the library on a Friday night when Lisa received a call and she had to leave urgently. She had packed a bag which Amit had made fun of for being garishly embroidered. While she got up to leave, her bag fell open and a leotard body suit fell out. He had looked at her quizzically, expecting a response but she had quickly gathered up the piece of clothing, a sad smile was her only explanation so far as she sped off. She came back the next day pretending everything was alright and they never spoke of the incident ever again. How would he make her know that to him she was *Rajkumari;* a princess and that just like Aishwarya Rai he thought she was a *pari (fairy)* and could never do any wrong in his eyes?

The next week, she had called him her voice heavy with unshed tears "Amit please, where are you? I can't take this anymore!"

His heart had skipped in alarm, "Are you alright, Lisa what is wrong?"

"Come and get me, please just come and get me. I will answer your questions later."

"Where are you?" he had known, even before the question took leave of his lips he knew where she was. He had bounded down the stairs, not caring how fast he was jumping and the possible injury he could get. He got to the club; she was lying down by the back entrance clutching her torn clothes to her slight frame. Her mascara was bleeding down her face in a stream of black from her continuous crying. A red haze slid over his vision as he watched her helpless form on the floor as she whimpered. He didn't need to ask her what had happened here, her appearance told the tale already. Without a word, he gathered her up in his arms and took her back to her room on campus while in his mind he called on recriminations upon everyone who had done this to her. Amit dropped her off with her roommate Zoya, a quiet Pakistani girl who he had met only once while he had come visiting Lisa. She took one look at her, nodded and took her inside dismissing Amit.

It took Amit days to get over the image of her broken and hurt, he could not bring himself to go see her for a week. Even when Zoya had called him saying she wanted to speak to him. He would not respond to her text messages or return her calls. When he had seemed to snap out of his depression and deep anger, he went to her place. She was lying in bed trying to study. He came in and stood wordlessly by the window for a long while as they stared each other down.

"My father's cement factory business had just collapsed," she began suddenly, not looking up at him while she fiddled with her hands in her lap. "He had declared bankruptcy. We lost our house because he had mortgaged it to save the business. They had to take all the money in my college trust fund to get a roof over our head. I could not add to their problems, I was only granted a part scholarship and I could not afford much else." she said in a whisper, staring intently at Amit.

"I did what I had to do, Amit. I am very sorry you had to see me like that."

"It would not be the first time Lisa" he said, finally turning to look at her. She frowned, confusion etching lines on her forehead.

"What do you mean, Amit?"

"The day before we met officially, my friends and I went to the strip club and I saw you perform. I recognized you from class, but I did not want to say anything. I didn't want to embarrass you."

Lisa groaned then, burying her head in the crook of her left arm and sobbing. The sobs wrenched through her body as if trying to tear apart her fragile frame as she rocked herself and choked on her shame and sorrow. Amit stood there helplessly, not knowing what to do to make her better. Tears had always scared the heck out of him.

"Please don't cry Lisa, its okay." Amit said to her softly, hovering by her bed and hesitating to touch her. He could not help still being old fashioned that way. "You do not need to be ashamed. I of all people understand lack. I only wish you had trusted me with this knowledge"

"I never wanted you to see me like that," she whispered brokenly still shielding her face.

"Its fine, I lo…. I like you still."

"Really?" her hopeful glance broke his heart.

"Yes, really. It would never change the way I see you" he went to her then, holding her and trying to offer comfort the way he knew how. That incident made their friendship stronger.

The last week of the semester, something strange happened. Amit was in the Gelman library studying when Mr. Patel, his professor approached him and sat down. He was shocked and worried. Mr. Patel was a Muslim Indian who was strict and principled; he always wore a white caftan with his hair slicked back from his always shining forehead. He was known for engaging students in arguments he termed 'captivating and interesting'. He had made the phrase; "do you reckon…" a notorious one in the computer science faculty because of his overuse of the phrase. Amit was really worried when he approached him, he wondered if he had done badly in the class quiz or if Mr. Patel had found his conduct inappropriate in any way. It turned out to be neither, Amit found out. Mr. Patel had come to engage him in a discussion involving what he was studying in Computer Algorithms. Amit was able to hold his own in that conversation even when Mr. Patel gave his equally infamous intimidating glare to make him unsure of his points, but he stood his ground. When Mr. Patel was supposedly satisfied, he left him.

"I'll leave you to your studying Mr. Khanna, I would rather say I enjoyed parrying words with you, I hope we can have a rematch?" he smiled and left without waiting for Amit's response. Amit could not help but feel like this was a test he had all but aced.

The next day, he got a letter from Mr. Patel's secretary summoning him to the man's lair. He entered Mr. Patel's office with trepidation, not sure what he would meet when he got in. Mr. Patel was sitting in his swivel chair reading a US journal issue and turning from side to side in the chair. The pose was so alien compared to Mr. Patel's usual appearance and composure, he had all but given them the notion that fun and relaxation was a leisure he could not afford and that anyone who still indulged them was unserious. When he shut the door as he entered, Mr. Patel slapped close the magazine he was reading and smiled at Amit...he smiled!!

"Sit down Mr. Khanna," the man said with a smile that kept widening. Amit had never seen Mr. Patel smile and they had come to believe that he was incapable of the expression. He sat down hesitantly on the edge of the seat, not getting used to having a seat with his superior except for disciplinary situations. Apparently, old habits and notions did die hard.

"How are you doing today, Mr. Khanna?" He asked him.

"Fine sir,"

"Do you know why you are here?" he asked still smiling hard. If his intentions were to put Amit at ease, he was doing a bad job of it.

"I suppose it has something to do with the discussion we had yesterday, sir."

"Good, yes Mr. Khanna. As a matter of fact, I had come to the library yesterday to look for materials for my research because I had run out of fresh ideas when I saw you reading on the subject. It seemed like a sign from Allah and I would be foolhardy to ignore it."

"What are you trying to say Sir?" he asked flummoxed.

"What I am saying my boy is that I need you on my research team. Our discussion has gone a long way in clearing the mental block in my mind. I would love to work with you… as a research assistant." Amit gazed at him more befuddled than before. Why would Mr. Patel want him on his team? He knew very little about Computer Algorithms, his major was computer engineering and programming. He had an interest in Computer Algorithms but not enough to major it plus he was not in his final year, research assistants were always in their final year in school or graduate assistants.

"But sir, I'm just a freshman. I would not…."

"Oh, I know Khanna," he said waving his hands at Amit as if to wave away his worries. "I can make an exception for you Mr. Khanna. I seem to think better around you Khanna, our conversation was very…. enlightening." he raised his eyebrows in an unspoken question. Amit was honored by the offer, but he was confused because he already worked for Ms. Sophia and he really liked working for her, so he told Mr. Patel his concerns.

"Don't worry Mr. Khanna, I would have you whenever you are free for 10$ an hour." Amit gaped at him, 10$!! It was getting better and better. He started to consider this offer too good to be true but then he considered that he would have nothing to lose if he took it.

"Alright Mr. Patel, I'll take your offer. Thank you for the opportunity sir."

"Good then, Mr. Khanna. I'll see you on Monday."

Amit left the office feeling like he had had a surreal experience. Lisa would be so happy for him. So, the year ended for Amit on a very good note. His parents would really be proud of him.

CHAPTER 3- THE WORLD IS COMING TO AN END

Amit found that holidays in a strange land without family was lonely. Most of the students had cleared out and gone home for the holidays and even the professors had gone home not needing their services anymore for the Christmas and New Year. Manoj had gone back to India to spend his vacation with family, Brian was in Cape Town with his missionary doctor parents and Min Ho had gone home to New Orleans. Lisa had invited Amit to come spend Christmas break with her family on the outskirts of Washington DC, but he had graciously declined her offer. As much as he wanted to be around people, he missed home around this time of the year and he really wanted to not impose himself on Lisa's parents. Add that to the fact that he was worried about what they might think of him and his relationship with their daughter. When he had told Lisa his concerns, she had laughed at him.

"Amit, you are so old fashioned it is almost funny! Who still thinks this way in this day and age?!" He was miffed that she was laughing at his expense, but he didn't care. He was who he was after all.

Since Ms. Sophia and Dr. Patel did not need his services during the holidays, he needed another job to fill his time and to save up for next year's rent and to augment whatever his parents were sending for his upkeep. He applied to a restaurant six miles from his apartment called 'the Joe Sacchin's Steak House' as a waiter and was employed. Most of the restaurants closer to school only had crowds in the evening because of some stragglers who had nowhere to go for the holidays and mostly came in for dinner and company. But the restaurants in downtown DC were usually full of customers at all given times of day because of family and friends that had come into town visiting and catching up. He was glad to be busy, so he would not have to feel lonely at the first end of the year holiday away from home.

Joe Sacchin's Steak House was really fancy and had a deck outside where you could sit and breathe in the clean Washington DC air. The interior must have been decorated by someone who loved Victorian era art. The floor was herring bone with a mix of dark and light woods. Tables edged the room with seats mostly facing the window, the aim obviously was to give them an excellent view of the busy sidewalk and the interesting people that walked by. The center also was littered with tables that at first looked like it had no particular design to it, but on closer look, you would find a concentric pattern that swirled and reminded Amit of that goddess thing in Moana. The ceiling was frangipani and was painted to look like the sea, so every time one looked up, you felt like you were under the sea. The counters were made of spotless white woo with clear glass showcasing mouthwatering pastries and the aroma coming from the kitchen could tempt a monk to break his fast or a strict Yogi to break his diet. Amit knew he would have never been able to afford eating in a restaurant like this on his budget and being in an environment like this afforded him the opportunity to be near good food. They served all kinds of oriental and Indian dishes, but Amit found he had acquired quite the taste for American food, especially the infamous cheeseburger and French fries.

This was where he met Anand, a shy, very religious, Indian boy. He was from Gujarat and he was a strict vegetarian which Amit found ironic and impressive. Impressive not because he didn't eat meat but that he could work in a steak house with all that sumptuous meat and still maintain his self-control. This topic seemed to be the anchor of their first ever discussion. They had been working the afternoon shift, Amit manning the counter, selling pastries and making drinks while Anand waited tables and filled out orders. They had been at it for a while when a beautiful middle-aged woman with an accent Amit could not quite place offered to buy Anand some rib eye steak, so he could sit and eat with her "for being so courteous" she had cited. Anand had quickly but politely declined which made Amit very curious. Their boss had no policy against his employers fraternizing with the customers if it didn't interfere with their work and technically, he could have taken his break then.

"Why did you not accept her offer?" Amit asked him at the end of their shift, his curiosity having the better of him. Anand looked up from tallying the orders he had filled and looked blankly at Amit.

"The nice lady who offered to buy you food; She was very nice."

Anand smiled slightly then, shaking his head, "I'm a vegetarian" he said simply with a shrug. Amit laughed then at the incredulity of it all.

"Why didn't you try to explain to her why you were declining? She seemed to have been slightly disappointed. Besides, you could have made sure she remained a customer for a very long time." Amit wiggled his brows at him suggestively. It earned him a laugh, a very boisterous laugh that burst out of Anand's mouth like a prisoner long awaiting release. He laughed so loud and for so long the cook had to come out and ask what the matter was. That stopped the both immediately.

"Are you Gujarati by chance?" Amit asked him still snickering. Anand nodded, coughing and the mirth still dancing in his eyes. "You Gujaratis are so weird," Amit continued still chuckling, "would it be so horrible to make chapattis the regular way? You have to stuff it with lentils and have a side of lentils too."

Anand laughed even harder, "You are just unbelievable. Sweet lentils actually taste better than beef soaked in gravy." He turned his nose up in disgust for extra effect. They laughed all the way home that day, parting at the junction that led to Amit's apartment. On their way home, he found out that Anand was Hindu and he was not an immigrant, his parents had migrated to America when they just got married so he could join a pharmacy research company that created wonder pills to help boost metabolism and made people lose weight. His mother had found a job as a teacher and Anand was a second-year student in GW University studying Computer Science. They discussed how strange it was that they had not ever run into each other in the CS department complex. Amit told Anand about his experience with Mr. Patel, they laughed at his persuasion skills and talked about how it was still evident that Indians did not really trust Americans with their businesses, so they would rather pick an inexperienced Indian to do the job. They talked till late into the night that day and when they did part, they were fast friends. From that day, they were inseparable.

This friendship was what made the great difference in Amit's prospectively lonely holiday. His life in India had been full of friends, loved ones, extended family and the likes. The parties were always numerous this time of year and there was always dancing. Amit had never been a great dancer, but he enjoyed watching his sister and cousins swaying to the beat of the drums and singing about love, loss, friendship, reverence to the Gods and family. His first Christmas holiday in America proved not to be so bad after all. They went to clubs together and danced to any song as long as the music was catchy. Most of the clubs in DC played hip-hop and DC was dominated by a lot of African- Americans. Most of the people worked really hard during the week so that they could spend money on the weekends. A lot of money was spent on weekends and entertainment was a huge part of their lifestyle. There was a lot of planning done to make sure that the weekend time was spent wisely; be it clubbing, sports, outdoor adventure or traveling. It was considered a sin to waste your weekend as the work week was monotonous and boring.

They drank eggnogs on New Year's Eve and watched the fireworks from the roof of Anand's apartment complex while laughing at the contagious excitement of Americans for things like New Year's Eve and the simplicity of their holidays compared to all the color and fuss of Indian celebrations.

When school began, Min Ho came back and announced that he was transferring to a school in Korea because his father had decided he needed to get closer to his roots. According to Min Ho, his words had been; "you need to get a little 'grounding', you seem a little untethered to me son." At this Manoj had laughed so hard Amit was afraid he would tear a muscle or hurt an organ and he told him as much which brought on more laughter.

"Your father needs to be oriented to the generation and century son," Manoj had said faking a British accent and turning his nose up like a spoilt debutante. Min Ho laughed then, for the first time since he came back from Christmas break.

"We would miss you Bro," Brian said. He moved out within the month and they found a new guy named Gaurav to move in and help with the bills. He was Gujju, and it became a point of duty for all three of them and Anand –who had become quite a fixture in their home- to tease him, calling him several weird names of meals the Gujarati were known for. "D*hokla*" was Brian's all-time favorite and it annoyed Gaurav to no end. He got used to the teasing and accepted it as his own form of hazing. Lisa was the only one who never got used to the teasing and always stood up for Gaurav when she visited.

The rest of the school year went away without much event.

Amit was enjoying his 1st year anniversary in America and enjoying the life style. His grades were good, had a good mix of friends and had a little bit of income from the 2 jobs. Life was good and then this happened.

Amit had been in their kitchen trying to fix himself some breakfast before going to the campus (Ms. Sophia was taking classes for new students and had retained Amit for extra pay much to the displeasure of Ravi) for work. On a rush of nostalgia, Amit had decided to make *upma* which was the Indian version of semolina. He had missed his mother's cooking and he would have killed to have homemade *upma* right about then. His culinary skills had been very limited while growing up because there had been so many females to do it coupled with the fact that his father believed there were 'more important' things for his son to do. So, his attempts at making himself a traditional and nostalgic breakfast were fast turning into an exercise in folly which was very frustrating. He was just about to give up on that too when he got a call from Anand.

"Where are you, Amit?" he asked with a strange sense of urgency Amit had never heard in his voice since he met him.

"I'm in the kitchen, is there a problem?"

"Turn on your TV." He hung up then as if he could not bear witnessing Amit's reaction to whatever he was trying to show him. With his heart in his throat, Amit turned on the television and saw the whole World in chaos. However urgent Anand had sounded on the phone, it had not prepared Amit for what he saw on the screen. He had thought about some really horrifying possibilities, but he had not been prepared for the images he saw on the screen; of people burnt beyond recognition being lifted out of the ruins of one of America's greatest tourist attractions. The news anchor on one of the news channels looked uncomfortable and in a concerned tone delivered the news; "An air plane has crashed into one of the twin towers located in New York City. We cannot confirm whether this is a terrorist attack at this point." Behind her frame, stretchers bearing the limp forms of men, women and children trooped out of the World Trade Center which was not a trade center anymore but a carnage scene.

As Amit stood before the screen, his blood curdling he prayed no one he knew was in that area even as a part of him wondered what this would mean for him. Manoj called him then, his voice a broken whisper of uncertainty as they tried to make sense of the madness that had overtaken their sane World. In heart and mind, they seemed to have banded together in this time; two brothers driven into a corner by a danger they were very ignorant of till then. He dressed in that state of panic and disconnection and started rushing to the university campus, the only thing on his mind to be around other people as he processed the news he had just heard. Probably someone who was as uncertain of their fate in this chaotic America they had found themselves in. Even if that company included Ravi, Amit found he did not mind as Ravi himself was in a way his brother. The old adage "misery loves company" took on a new meaning for Amit that day.

The streets were in turmoil, even the homeless guy Barry who lived on the end of Amit's street who always had jokes, news and anecdotes for people and had developed quite the fondness for Amit was not left out. The ever-cheerful man whom Amit looked forward to seeing each morning was screaming hysterically at the top of his lungs as people rushed past him. "The World is coming to an end! The World is coming to an end!" he screamed, pumping his fists in the air. Amit prayed this sight would not stay in his mind.

He got to work to see Ms. Sophia locking up while Ravi stood helplessly by her side and people trooping by them as if trying to make up their mind about where they should be at that time. Ms. Sophia took one look at Amit and dismissed him with a wave of her hand as she rushed to get into her 2015 model BMW and zooming off. Ravi cast a disproving look at Amit as if he caused the misfortune and had upset their employer, but Amit was not even paying him any mind.

Amit got home to realize his phone had been ringing off the hook. It was his family; they must have heard from the news what was going on and were worried about his safety. When his mother heard his voice, she broke down crying in relief as she thanked lord Shiva for preserving the life of her only son. He spoke to them for a while, reassuring his parents and granny that he was unharmed but confused. In all his years in America, Amit would never forget September 11th. The day the World was lit up in flames.

CHAPTER 4 - OFF KILTER

Amit woke up the next day to a World that was never quite the same. It was normal for the equilibrium of things to be upset for a while after the bombing of the World trade center and the Pentagon, but it felt to Amit like the scale was spun out of control and could not quite remember what its balance point was. Amit woke up the next day to the American president George W. Bush on all TV and news stations trying to pacify and reassure an already agitated and unsure people. The terrorist sect *Al Qaeda* was suspected of the coordinated and repeated attacks and he was sure to inform them that further investigations were ongoing. Other reporters had a field day, informing the public of the number of deaths, injuries and the damage to the American people. By the third day, the deaths were around two thousand, six hundred and sixty-nine with over six thousand people injured among which were four hundred and fifteen dead law enforcement agents at both the World Trade Center and the headquarters of the United States Department of Defense; the Pentagon in Arlington county Virginia. These numbers were burned into Amit's skull and every time he closed his eyes he was presented with the images of those limp bodies and charred remains he had seen on TV. Amit prayed they found peace in their next life. He made an offering to Lord Shiva, thanking him for protection and guidance. Then he prayed for the peace and prosperity of himself and his family, so they would not be victims in any case like this.

By the start of the next session, Amit noticed the subtle shift in behavior of the people around them. He used to think America was a place where you could lose who you really were if you wanted, where you could be anything you wanted, and it was ok. But he had come to realize that was never going to be true. The illusion of obscurity was shattered for him because he found that now, they would not let him forget who and what he was. He was first a foreigner before he was anything else, and right now he was the foreigner who reminded them of the numerous deaths of their loved ones; relatives, fathers, mothers, sisters, brothers, children, friends and spouses. He tried to ignore it, but how could you ignore something that smacked you in the face every time you looked up? It was hard to ignore the fact that people who would normally greet you with a smile when you passed by them now would pointedly ignore you when you walked past, and they would make a point of avoiding eye contact and avoiding your path. The homeless guy Barry had no greeting for Amit or his kin anymore. He used to throw out greetings to everyone who walked past him and a special greeting for Amit, he even learned how to say *Namaskar* in Hindi to show Amit his goodwill. But now, he pretended he was much occupied with whatever he was doing that he would not have to acknowledge Amit as he passed by. At first, before Amit came to realize that he was in the middle of a cold war of sorts, he would shout a greeting to Mr. Barry.

"Good morning Barry, *Namaskar*" he would clasp his hands together in his face and would drop the occasional treat at Mr. Barry's space, but he would not look up. Until he found out his treats were left in the exact same spot without being touched. Even Ms. Sophia became abrupt and curt with him and Ravi, but the guy was as clueless as a dolt. All these brought home the point that it had become a very difficult thing to be a man of color in the early twenty first century America. Brian moved out of their apartment without much explanation, his brother had been a firefighter and he had died in the rescue mission when the World trade center had collapsed after the fire. He had never been found. Brian had come back to school a ghost of his usually cheerful self, moping and drinking and attending parties. When Amit and Manoj had confronted him, he had treated them like they were invisible; he had looked through them and screamed for another drink. The next day, they came back to the house and he was nowhere to be found, his clothes had left with him too. That was the last they heard from him or saw him.

In 1996, Osama bin Laden the leader of Al Qaeda had traveled to Afghanistan and emboldened by the guidance of Ayman al-Zawahiri, had issued his first *fatwa* calling for American soldiers to leave Saudi Arabia. Then in 1998, he organized a second *fatwa* outlining his objections to American foreign policy with respect to their support of Israel as well as the continued presence of American troops in Saudi Arabia after the Gulf War. He exhorted and impelled Muslims with Islamic texts to attack Americans until the stated grievances are reversed. So it was no wonder that Al Qaeda was the first suspect of the coordinated attack against the Pentagon and the World Trade Center and also the failed attempt on the White House (the fourth plane, American Airlines Flight 93 was initially flown toward Washington, D.C. but it had crashed into field in Stony creek Township near Shanksville, Pennsylvania, after its passengers thwarted the hijackers). The United States quickly responded by launching the War on Terror and invaded Afghanistan to depose the Taliban, which had failed to comply with U.S demands to extradite Osama bin Laden and expel Al Qaeda from Afghanistan.

Emotions were on the rise, people were hurt and confused so they blamed the most convenient people to blame; immigrants. You could see the hate and recrimination in their eyes. As an immigrant now, one did not just have to worry about racists, one had to deal with the xenophobia that was becoming a thing in America. In a way Amit did not really blame them, they were reacting like wounded animals; hurt and confused, they lashed out the only ways they knew how. The Episcopalian church in Amit's neighborhood held several memorial masses that month for people who had been lost in the carnage. Enlarged pictures hung on large frames, with flower ornaments or the medals the deceased had won in life and in death (for the firefighters and NYPD). Everywhere he looked, Amit saw polished pictures, memorabilia and letters written to the dead frequently. It was as if they were trying to keep the memory of their grief and sorrow fresh.

What almost broke him was Lisa. She had lost her father in the West Tower on the 78th floor. He had gone to New York to get a business loan from the West Side Bank when the first plane had crashed into the West tower. His body had been the first to be found when the rescue team had gone in before the building collapsed on itself killing the firemen who had gone in for the rescue. They had had the memorial service at St. Peter's a church that had miraculously been spared from the carnage of the WTC even though it was situated very close to ground zero. Amit wanted to be with her on such a difficult time in her life, but she declined his company then, insisting that her family needed the time alone. He had respected her wishes.

She returned to school unannounced which was odd because she always told Zoya and Debbie her closest friend about her whereabouts. That seemed to be the least of their problems because after then she started to seem strange to her friends. Zoya said she had seemed unhinged to her.

"She seems strange Amit, I don't know how to help her," Zoya looked worried as she shared the news with Amit at a Breakfast Deli they all visited.

"Of course, she seems strange, Zoya she just lost her father! People handle grief differently"

"You don't understand Amit, she…..talks to herself and she rarely pays attention to anything around her anymore" her eyes darted round the café worriedly as if scared someone was witness to her snitching on her roommate and friend. "I'm really worried Amit, please come talk to her, she might listen to you."

"She won't even see me!" Amit raked a hand through his coffee colored hair in frustration. Lisa had been avoiding him since she came back. One shallow excuse after another whenever he tried to visit her or set time to study together. "I'm not ready Amit." She always said.

"Please Amit, just try." He sighed wearily. "Alright."

****

"At some point you would have to come out and speak to me Lisa" Amit said to the door, his forehead pressed against the door jamb of Lisa's apartment. Zoya had left the room in the morning and called Amit to let him know the coast was clear and he could come talk to her. So far, he had been standing at the door for over an hour and Lisa was totally ignoring him.

"Please Lisa, I know you are hurting but you need to talk to someone. Let us help you, let me help you." He whispered into the keyhole. "I miss my friend Lisa." Still, there was no response from her. He could hear her sobbing though, she was trying to muffle the sounds with a cloth or pillow but her sharp intake of breath and choking sounds still got out. This encouraged Amit and he knocked a little louder on the door.

"I would stay here all day and night if I have to Lisa. Till you're ready to speak to me." And he did stay, sitting on the floor with his back against the wall till it was dark and Zoya was home. Amit left that night feeling her loss like his own. He had been wrong when he said he had not lost anything in the attacks; he had lost his princess and he knew it would take a lot to have her back. He sought Anand out to share his woes and unfortunate luck in love.

"All will be well brother," Anand told him patting his shoulder lightly. "The Goddess of love is looking out for you two." Amit said nothing in response, he did not tell Anand he didn't feel like the Gods were ever looking out for him since he came to this land. He had not prayed so much nor made any offerings in the past year, but he did not tell Anand that either because he knew how much Anand believed and how devout he was. So, he just nodded, not the least bit encouraged by her words of supposed comfort.

After two weeks of trying and failing to get Lisa's attention, she came onto his radar. Amit was shocked beyond words could describe. She looked very different and Amit was not sure what to make of the change in her appearance. She had hacked her beautiful blond hair which Amit had loved and dubbed liquid gold that flowed to the small of her back. She had hacked it down to chin level and dyed it a reddish purple. She lined her eyes thickly with mascara and changed her clothes, now favoring dark colored jeans and leather pants and jackets to her former flower print dresses and bright cheerful blouses. She even went as far as getting a piercing in her upper lip and started wearing purple lipstick. His sweet princess was now a real Goth girl. But what hurt Amit most was the way she looked at him; like he was invisible, the scum of the earth and beneath her notice.

"If it isn't the smart brown boy!" she said one day when he tried to talk to her on the faculty corridors. "What do you want?" She leaned on the wall nonchalantly, rolling her eyes at his pleading gaze as two strange guys and a lady who were dressed in the same way as she lounged around waiting for her.

"Can we talk, please Lisa?" he asked in a low voice. She laughed then, loud and hoarsely which was very uncharacteristic for her.

"I'm afraid I don't have the time or patience for you and your antics. I am very busy." she flung the words at him with a flick of her wrist.

"This isn't you Princess," he whispered to her and her eyes hardened. "Don't you ever call me that again, ever! While I was besotted with a brown boy, letting the thoughts of you preoccupy me, my father was killed by your kind. So, excuse me if I want nothing to ever do with you again." The words poured out of her, spilling the pain she was trying to hide. The hatred in her eyes was a punch to Amit's gut.

"You are all the same;" she continued, "Vermin and plagues my country needs to get rid of." She left then, taking her crew with her leaving Amit standing in the open courtyard in the aftermath of her hurtful words. Not once in the exchange had she said his name or looked directly at his eyes. She could not even stand the sight of him and that was when Amit knew he had lost too to September eleventh. He had lost Lisa.

Amit was going to graduate, and this was the American labor market he was going to be thrust in. *It was anything but the right time to graduate* Amit thought to himself. He was not ready to face the possible hostility he would encounter with the strong waves of racism and xenophobia sweeping across the nation. His future was not certain, and he was scared, he had family obligations and he had a load of student loans to pay back and he didn't know how to go about finding his way. Amit would have loved to take additional courses at G-DUB, but with all the responsibilities resting on his shoulders, he needed to step up. This was his reality. The only problem he would run into now was the fact that he needed whichever company that would employ him to sponsor H-1B visa for him and this would not be an easy feat at all considering the Year 2000 fiasco (Y2K) that hit the Tech World as it was ushered into the new millennium and the September 11 tragedy the country was still recovering from.

Several tech company scouts had come to the school to recruit Java and C++ developers but none of them were willing to sponsor H-1B visa as the process and resource that went into it were too much and many American companies were not willing to put in that much time and resource for someone that could be a flight risk. Plus, the waiting time for a response from the United States Citizenship and Immigration Services (USCIS) was too long and it was not certain the visa would be approved.

Amit and Anand had found new studio apartment little ways from the steakhouse where they had met, and they had asked Joe to help them with jobs which he was eager to do. "They don't find hard workers like you on the streets anymore," he had told them. "I would be glad to let you fill the Barista's position. Amit, he is going to college soon. Anand, could wait tables again, Stacy can't do it alone anyway."

They were grateful for his help, but Anand could not help pointing out how eager he was to take them on because they were known to work really hard. Indians generally were considered to be quality labor provided at a very cheap rate. They were mostly known to do excellent computer work and also good with numbers. There was a saying that if you needed a trusted cab driver or tech guy for your computers, contact an Indian guy. "Congratulations Amit," Anand said wryly. "We have become a stereotype." His laughter rang out loud and clear as they walked home.

"Come to think of it, he does mean well" Amit said with a straight face.

"Oh, I know his heart is in the right place, but that heart is so big it would contain us all; Indians, Chinese, French…" Amit laughed out loud then, punching Anand in the arm. Anand's dry, sarcastic humor always made Amit laugh. He would make fun of certain details about the people they had met, seeming serious but it was all just pretense, and Amit had to go along with it till he couldn't any longer and he cracked up. Amit knew Anand held no ill will towards Joe Sacchin's, but he could not help pointing out their reality in self-deprecating humor.

Amit was sleeping in one morning; his shift at Joe's was for the evening so he decided to take some time to rest from the job hunt when Anand woke him with a slap of whatever paper he was reading.

"Wake up, lazy bones. You have to see this!" Amit groaned and pulled the pillow up over his head, turning away from the light Anand was letting into his room.

"I'm done, Bud" he mumbled with his face still buried in his pillow. The words sounded like 'I don't want to' to Anand but he wasn't so sure. He hit him harder with the newspaper grumbling about his sleeping habits. With an exasperated sigh, Amit got up, knowing Anand would not stop till he finally got his attention.

"It better be good, whatever this is." He said staggering to the breakfast corner and fixing himself some cereal while Anand watched in dismay.

"You won't brush or wash up first?" Anand asked clearly troubled by the prospects. Amit ignored him and continued to spoon sugar into his cereal. He was really enjoying Anand's discomfort, if the man was going to wake him from sleep for any reason at all, he had to be able to put up with his sloppy behavior and lacking hygiene. Anand was a neat freak, Amit had asked him if he was sure he was not obsessive compulsive at the beginning of their friendship. He was so particular and principled about the things he did; and not taking a bath or even just washing up before breakfast was an anathema for him. Amit knew these things and was really glad he was riling him up.

"You are just disgusting." Anand shook his head at Amit dismissively and placed the newspaper before Amit, folding it out to a page.

"Do you need a job as a computer programmer or technician? Are you a fresh Indian graduate in search of a good job? We at E.B.IT Consulting firm would love to connect you to the job of your dreams for 50$ an hour. We would also be willing to process H-1B visa for you. If interested, contact the numbers below." Amit read the ad out loud, looking at Anand quizzically.

"Is this real?" he asked.

"We would have to find out" Anand shrugged, looking at him intently.

"The pay is not so great though" Amit scrunched up his nose. Anand laughed out loud then.

"Are you serious now Amit? This is the best deal we could get! You are not even paid $50 for the whole day at Joe's but we were grateful for that job. Why is this one so bad?"

"It is a Desi consulting company; their methods are not ethical." Amit replied still skeptical.

"Who cares, Amit? This is America! And jobs are hard to come by for us with everything going on. This is our only opportunity to get paid some real money and still do what we love doing." His voice was going up a notch as he tried to persuade Amit. "It does not get better than this, at least for a while. We have responsibilities and obligations to fulfill with only tips from waiting tables as our source of income. How do you intend to pay off all your student loans?"

This was what weakened Amit's resolve; he hated remembering all the financial obligations he had. His mom had called yesterday, talking about finding a suitor for his sister Pooja and the dowry was seven hundred thousand Indian Rupees which was equivalent to $10,000. She had not made any requests, but it had been implied that his parents expected him to step in and contribute to Pooja's marriage. Plus, his student loans, always the student loans. He had been on a partial scholarship that had covered only half of his tuition. His father had taken loans to pay the rest and he had heard how those loans would rack up interest if he did not pay up on time.

A desi (run by people of Indian/Pakistani/ Bangla) consulting company was a consulting firm dealing with the employment of foreign Indians in America especially for computer sciences and technology. They would help get you a job and then take a percentage of your income, possibly even the bigger margin of your income. The only good thing about them was that they would sponsor your H-1B visa and process permanent residency which was a good deal. It was wrong though, but many foreign young graduates were signing up with them because of the notion that no one else would hire them. These companies would even help organize interviews for the main employers, impersonating and copying a qualified person's portfolio, hence allowing for the employment of some unqualified people in these companies. This was contributing to the problem of computer science graduates not being able to find decent jobs. Amit considered this seriously and decided he would be the change he wanted to see in the World, only if he had not starved to death from hunger.

"Are you sure about this Anand?" he asked again.

"Of course, brother," Anand replied with a smile. And with that they were sold on the idea. He made plans to call the consulting company the next day.

CHAPTER 5- HIGH ON H1B VISA

The next morning, Amit called the number they had found on the Desi company ad. He was still quite skeptical and had told Anand as much. "If they sound unconvincing in any way, I would totally hang up and forget this idea."

"Nothing ventured, nothing gained." Anand had only shrugged and said. The phone rang for a while, and just as Amit was about to hang up, a lady picked up. Her voice was sultry, did these people think they could get young graduates interested with the implied promise of carnal pleasure? Amit shook his head, shooting Anand an enigmatic look.

"This is E.B. consulting company, what can I do for you?" she drawled throatily, and it made Amit cringe.

"Err yes, my name is Amit Khanna, I saw the ad you placed in the newspaper calling for students on OPT who needed jobs. I'm interested."

"Oh yes, Mr. Khanna, I am Emily the human relations officer at E.B. and we could schedule your interview right now if you would like?"

"Yes, yes of course ma'am. Any day would be fine by us."

"Us?"

"Yes, I am asking for my friend and me ma'am." She chuckled then, "Well tell your friend that we would love you two to come in on Monday morning by 7 a.m. for the interview."

"Would you mind telling us what is expected of us during the interview?" she laughed then, "It's just a formality Mr. Khanna, and we would only ask technical and behavioral questions. Those should be easy for you to crack, wouldn't it?"
"Why yes, of course ma'am, thank you very much."

"You are welcome Mr. Khanna, we'll be expecting you." Amit nodded as if she could physically see him. But then he wanted to clear more doubts.

"Excuse me ma'am, one more question. Would your company really sponsor H-1B visa for your employees?"

"Of course, Mr. Khanna," she said sounding amused. "We also make provisions for sponsorship of a permanent residence card." Just like that, Amit was totally sold on them.

The H-1B is a visa in the United States under the Immigration and Nationality Act, section 101(a)(15)(H) which allows U.S. employers to employ foreign workers in specialty occupations. If a foreign worker in H-1B status quits or is dismissed from the sponsoring employer, the worker must either apply for and be granted a change of status, find another employer (subject to application for adjustment of status and/or change of visa), or leave the United States. The regulations define a "specialty occupation" as one requiring theoretical and practical application of a body of highly specialized knowledge in a field of human endeavor including but not limited to biotechnology, chemistry, computing, architecture, engineering, statistics, physical sciences, journalism, medicine and health: doctor, dentists, nurses, physiotherapists, etc., economics, education, research, law, accounting, business specialties, technical writing, theology, and the arts, and requiring the attainment of a bachelor's degree or its equivalent as a minimum. Likewise, the foreign worker must possess at least a bachelor's degree or its equivalent and state licensure, if required to practice in that field. H-1B work-authorization is strictly limited to employment by the sponsoring employer.

Most of these students came on F-1 visa (some of them immigrated to United States on Green Card) and the short-term goal for them was to get the H-1B visa to buy time for permanent residency. Most of these Indian consulting firms worked with a good law firm and had negotiated fees with the firm for H-1B visas and I-140 applications (Immigration Petition for an Alien worker) in bulk. The administrative office of these consulting firms had a fantastic relationship with the lawyer's office. Like mafia is run on death threats, consulting firms were run on the fear of visas and green cards. Companies used the visas and pending green cards to retain employees. The permanent residency/green card process was lengthy and took as much as 5 to 8 years (sometimes more). H-1B visa could keep someone in the country for up to 7-8 years (It had two 3-year periods and two 1-year extensions). Once an employee started the green card process with one employer, he or she preferred staying with that employer since changing the job would start the application process from scratch. Also, law offices knew that this was a perfect source of recurring revenue for them. One student from a foreign country made from 10k to 15k for the law offices and a good mid-size consulting firm had around 80-100 consultants. Although Americans did not like immigrants a whole lot, they spent a lot of money to boost U.S economy and at the same time were hard-working and skilled.

It turned out that the HR manager for E.B. was right. The interview turned out to be just ceremonial. Amit and Anand were hired on the spot. They were required to sign a non-binding contract; the contract said that E.B. Consulting Firm would market both to find a position for them. And once they were on the client site, they would have to work with the company for 18 months and if they left the company before that, the liability of 25,000 USD was paid for the training and accommodation expenses provided by E.B. Consulting. The deal was not the best, but it was not like they had a choice. This was why the firm was trying to sweeten the deal by sponsoring their permanent residency application.

They put in their resignation at Joe Sacchin's because they were needed to start their IT training for the consulting company in preparation for the job placement.   Amit had heard it said that many guys had applied for the job with the consulting company but only three of them had been selected; Amit, Anand and another Indian guy named Sandeep. Amit could not figure out what it was about them that had made them so special that they were chosen over these other guys who had applied for the job. But you didn't look a gift horse in the mouth; Amit had learned that as a valuable lesson from his mom.

They had an option to move into a guest house provided by the company while they did their IT training and processed their H1-B visa. This seemed like a sort of insurance for their employers to make sure they were in a controlled environment and did not change their mind during the duration of training, but Amit was not sure about this as there were a lot of unethical things about this company.

The training provided by the consulting firm was quite easy for Amit, it was not so different from his discipline in school but instead of learning algorithms from Professors, he was learning software testing and business analysis from these trainers with Punjabi accent in a classroom with software that looked subpar. Training included concepts of software testing, tools used by various companies, software business analysis and the tools used to conduct business analysis. The trainer's name was Mr. Sharma. He was a 65-year-old gentleman who had been a computer teacher in a Government school in India. His Punjabi accent was still very heavy and thick, and he still tripped on the consonants like the 'f' and 'v' pronouncing them with his upper and lower lips instead of with the upper teeth and lower lip. He used the common phrases like 'chak de phatte' which was like the phrase 'hitting the ball out of the park' used in America a whole lot. 'Very fat was pronounced as 'bery phat'. Amit admired the fact that he was not a wannabe like most Indians who came to America taking on a fake accent and pretending to be better than everyone else. He appreciated the man's teaching style and his easy allusion to Indian culture and roots while teaching, but it was evident to anyone who cared to look that Mr. Sharma was barely qualified for this job he had taken on. The man seemed to be struggling with getting a grip on the advanced software testing courses he was taking on and when it seemed to overwhelm him, he resorted to telling them stories about his children and grandchildren back in India and how his granddaughter Amrita loved cats so much she took in stray cats where she could and the house was over populated. By the end of the first month, they knew so much about him and very little about what he had come to teach them.

On the first day of class, Mr. Sharma had come into the classroom with his bundle of notes which were copies of software manuals and help files of the various testing and business analysis tools, shuffling under the weight of them. He had plopped the books down and in the form of an introduction, had asked the question; "What is the job of a good software tester?" Amit had responded confident in his knowledge and the chance to make an impression on the man. "To test the system comprehensively and discover any defects as a result of that."

Mr. Sharma had quickly shaken his head, "No, to find bugs. Don't use that many words son." Everyone in the class had roared in laughter, finding his antics funny. Amit's answer had been accurate and better than Mr. Sharma's but the man had no professional grasp of the concepts. "You see, my son Amit loves making very simple things complex too. That is an easy skill to have," he had said looking intently into their faces and pointing. "But making the complex simple, ridiculously simple, that is a very rare and great talent." All his lectures covered basic concepts for a person to get an entry level job as a tester.

To say Amit was disappointed would be putting it mildly, "You would think that they'd get qualified personnel to train us for the job interview since they would be earning from our pays but no!" he sulked to Anand and Sandeep as they lounged in the living room of the guesthouse they shared, drinking glasses of fresh milk 'taaza doodh' that Sandeep had bought on his way from the local oriental market where fresh Asian food produce were sold. Anand chuckled and continued to type away on his computer savoring every sip of his milk like it was a rare treat which it could well be.

"To be fair to him, his classes are quite interesting," Sandeep said, Amit scowled at his halfhearted attempt at a joke. Sandeep was a computer science major from UCLA. He was from Delhi and he was married with two kids back home. He had come to America seeking greener pastures for his family. He wanted to obtain a steady job and a permanent residency before sending for his family to come join him here. He was in his early thirties with an angular face chiseled like a warrior God. The man had a dry self-deprecating sense of humor and he seemed to find mirth even in the most horrible of situations. This lent to his charm and that humor seemed to be needed now because Amit was on a roll, and when Amit got like this, Anand carefully extracted himself from the offending situation till he calmed down.

"I would call them out in the morning about the quality of this training." Amit said as a promise to no one in particular, probably to himself. It seemed that resolve made him feel a bit better because his engine let off a considerable amount of steam after then. Sandeep exchanged a meaningful look with Anand and they chuckled. Anand loved Amit like a brother, but sometimes his high-handed expectations of perfection from everyone and everything seemed to put a pressure on him and the people around him. He had unbending rules about things in life; it was all black and white to him. He had tried to tell him on several occasions to give space and credence to all the shades of grey in life, that it was not so clear cut all the time. Sandeep found his hot headedness very entertaining and tolerated his antics like that of a truculent teenager.

Amit did initiate a complaint about Mr. Sharma the very next day to the training resource person, Mr. James Wilson. He was an Indian who fancied himself American. He claimed he was biracial, and his father was from Manhattan, but he was as brown as they come, and no one knew enough to refute his claims, so they let him alone. When he heard Amit's concerns, he tried to pacify him by pointing out that they had H-4 visa holders (wives of H1b visa holders) who had no technical background at all in the class with them, so the lectures had to be rudimentary for them to grasp the concepts easily and be able to pass the interviews.

"Besides, we know this course is just a formality for you. You just need to present a certificate proving that you had a training in Information Technology." He gave Amit a sticky smile that roiled his stomach. What was the point of the whole exercise if they could just print fake certificates and give them to present? Amit worked his jaw repeatedly biting on his tongue as if trying to swallow unpleasant words. When he seemed to be under control, he stormed out of his office, deciding not to attend any of those classes again.

****

Sandeep sighed as he listened to Sanjana talk. "Ma and Pratik are always asking me when you will come to take us Sandeep, the neighbors are talking," her voice broke as she muttered into the phone. He could picture her taking the land line extension into their room and whispering so his parents and their kids do not overhear them.

"I'm trying my best Sanjana," he was weary, and he knew he sounded it. They had had this conversation repeatedly for over three years since he graduated from college here in America. He had been trying to land a job here in America and get his green card ever since but nothing had panned out. He had tried everything; he had worked as a sales clerk in a department store, he had sold tickets at the stadium for 50 cents, he had worked as a janitor at a hotel all this while waiting for something to click so he could get his family to join him over here.

"I would get you everything you deserve, Sanjana." He had promised her before he left and every time since then; "we would have a grand life; our kids would not want quality education."

With every year that passed, the promises had become; "It will only just take a little more time Sanju, we will be together very soon!" but every time he made that promise, it sounded hollower to both their ears. He was not closer to fulfilling it now than he was three years ago. Now he didn't even make the promise anymore, he didn't know what to tell his family. He could picture his 7-year-old son Pratik with caramel colored eyes so like his own and the innocent inquisitiveness that was not out of place for a boy his age asking when papa would come take them to be with him in 'uhmerika'. He had been just a baby when Sandeep had left and his daughter Bashu was three then. Now she was eleven and was not as eager to come to the phone to speak to him anymore. Frustration stabbed at his heart, he had let his hunger for the American dream steal his family away from him. He could not help counting his losses for this mirage he was chasing that kept slipping from his grasp. What grieved him more was the fact that he could not stop now, he was too far in, had lost so much already to just go back home. And he did not even have enough money for a plane ticket back to India.

Sanjana's soft sobs pulled him up from the pit of self-pity he was fast slipping into. "Sanju, please don't cry" his voice was hoarse with his own unshed tears. "How would you look with kohl dripping down your eyes like Gauri huh?" she uttered a halfhearted laugh in response to his attempts at humor. Gauri was a Bollywood horror movie they had seen together where the ghost always had kohl dripping down her face like a drag queen who had been in the rain.

"I'm not wearing kohl today." She said sniffing.

"What?" he shouted in mock indignation, "My wife now goes about without making herself pretty because I am not home? That is totally unacceptable!" She giggled then like a school girl, the sound like a soothing balm to Sandeep's soul.

"You don't think I am pretty without adornments?" she asked coyly, knowing what would come next. "Oh, I think you are very beautiful *my love*, I that's how you bewitched me and kept me pining after you"

She sighed then, and he could somehow hear the smile in her voice then. "I will try my very best Sanju, if that is the last thing I do." He vowed then strongly to her in the heat of his emotions.

"You promise?" she asked softly.

"By Lord Ram, I swear it" he replied.

"I believe you." She whispered. "I will wait" they said their goodbyes then, so she could go bring their children back from school and he hung up. Sandeep sighed again, the weight of Sanjana's blind faith in him weighing heavy on his shoulders. He vowed then he would do anything to get that green card even if he died trying. His resolve was strengthened now; he remembered who he was doing this for. He would do anything to bring his family together again.

CHAPTER 6 – DOLLAR, DOLLAR, DOLLAR

Amit sat in the coffee shop close to the metro station in DC and watched as people walked past. He rubbed his hands on the sides of the coffee mug holding his decaf latte which tasted almost like fresh milk. He chuckled to himself as he looked down into the cup of 'milk' he was drinking. His father would cringe if he knew what Amit was drinking. His father preferred strong brews of coffee, and he loved it black. "Nothing says man up like a strong cup of black coffee" his father would say. But he never had acquired the taste for the bitter, black thing. He had hated coffee as a matter of fact till he started studying with Lisa, and she had introduced him to decaf lattes which became an acquired taste that had quite grown on him. He sighed then at the memory of her; his Lisa with the sweet smile that could light up a room and cheer up an old man. He had not tried to contact her since that day in the faculty corridors when she had looked at him with so much hate, associating him with her grief but he had not forgotten her, not by a long shot. He still wondered what had become of her if she had finally gotten past her hurt and moved on.

On a whim, he had felt like jumping on a bus and going to Jersey Shore to look for her, he remembered all the stories she had told about that place; the salty sea breeze, the waves crashing in the distance the only sound you heard early in the morning most days if you were an early riser, the seagulls quaking in perfect symphony. She had made him feel guilty and silly for missing that Christmas with her family and she had weaseled a promise out of him that he would come visit with her the next summer. That day never came for them. September eleventh had happened, and most people's lives had gone on a stand still. It had been three years, but it still felt like September twelfth for many people who had lost something or someone in that great terrorist attack.

The US had done a lot of investigations into *Al Qaeda* and Osama bin Laden since that time and all evidence pointed to the fact that he was the instigator of those attacks. In November 2001, the United States forces recovered a videotape from a destroyed house in Jalalabad, Afghanistan. In the video, Bin Laden was seen talking to Zavari and had admitted previous knowledge of the attacks. In December 27th, 2001, a second video was found, in the video he had extolled terrorism against America because of their conceived hatred for Islam and their support for the Israeli people. But shortly before the U. S presidential election in 2004, bin Laden used a taped statement to publicly acknowledge al-Qaeda's involvement in the attacks on the United States. He admitted his direct link to the attacks and stated the motives for them. He said he had personally directed the attacks on the World Trade Centre and the Pentagon saying they were carried out because; 'we are free…. and want to regain freedom for our nation. As you undermine our security, we undermine yours.'

Now people could put a definite face to the cause of their grief and Amit wondered if it was good for them. Because it seemed that some victims who now had a name and a face got stuck still, obsessing over the whys and if onlys. He had heard of a man in New York who had lost his father and three brothers who were firefighters in the tower, after hearing the admission of guilt by bin Laden, had gone to the Pakistani embassy and opened fire, shooting randomly till he was gunned down. Another life stuck in the past and the grief of 9/11 that had finally let the pain consume him. Amit hoped Lisa was well, his heart had stopped hurting so much when he thought about her, it had taken time, but the pain had dulled to a sore ache in the center of his chest that he could ignore most of the time till he remembered that it was still supposed to hurt. The pain had become like an old friend, and he could not but welcome it.

He rubbed his chest absently now, enjoying the reprieve he had taken for himself today. The training they were taking at E.B. was becoming a grind and he was not interested in listening to Mr. Sharma prattle on more about his family than about software testing. He had stormed out of Mr. James Wilson's office the day before, after making his complaint and getting the weak defense they had to give- fuming at the mouth, hating the system and its rotten methods of administration. Last week, they had been introduced to the marketing team who would place the employees and they assisted the graduates to customize their resume so that the placement was easier. The marketing department however were looking for the more promising ones who had a decent education, had good communication skills, good grasp of the English language and had good basic technical skills. Amit, Anand and Sandeep had all of these and they were awaiting placement, the ones who would have a problem getting placed were the wives of the H-1B visa holders who had no technical or computer education whatsoever and had limited grasp of the English language. Hence the rudimentary lectures being given by Mr. Sharma and the other tutors. There were also a few guys in their training batch who had little or no education and technical skills too, one of them was Gowan Deepak a very shy, very quiet guy who never said anything in those classes. From what Meghna, one of the H-4 wives had said; Gowan was an electrician who had a natural inclination for what he did but he needed a green card within 6 months. So, he was here by the help of one of the marketing team members, a guy Amit had only seen once during the introduction.

Amit had taken a mild interest in Gowan Deepak when he noticed he never once spoke in the class and even outside it, he wondered if the man ever spoke at all or if he just was not comfortable speaking in front of people he did not feel at home with. That was until Mr. Sharma had asked him a direct question some days ago in class and the guy could not make a coherent speech in English language. He kept stammering and jerking his head about, speaking Hindi all through. Everyone in the class had laughed, well almost everyone because Amit did not find it funny. Even Gowan had laughed, exhibiting some sort of self-deprecating humor that was uncharacteristic of him, but Amit would not know what was in character for him because he had not gotten to know Gowan and thus didn't know what kind of a sense of humor he had, if any. Amit could easily see himself in Gowan, true, he did have a little aptitude for the English language and he was gifted with an inclination for the sciences, but he had had a very horrible stage fright and could never stand and talk to any audience past three persons in a formal setting without making a fool of himself. He remembered the very first ever class presentation he had to give; it was an oral class quiz in Professor Sackman's class where everyone was required to answer some questions within a certain time and the marks were judged by the speed and accuracy with which you answered. When it was his turn, his tongue had twisted up on itself, refusing to cooperate with him and his brain had gone on a mini vacation on him. The one hour allocated for his viva was the worst one hour of his existence in GW University. He had flunked that test woefully and if it had not been for Lisa's timely intervention, his grades would have suffered. She had helped him learn to speak to intimidating crowds and hold his own amongst them. *"For you to overcome your fear of speaking to a large crowd Amit, you have to rehearse before an even scarier audience"* she had said with a cheeky smile. He had not understood what she meant until she took him to the subway station and asked him to recite his words out loud, not minding who was listening or looking at him. He had been scared but he had done it, one among the crazy things he and Lisa had done together. He frowned thoughtfully while looking into the distance, this sudden avalanche of memories of Lisa and their time together was making him uncomfortable. He could not figure out why his brain had decided to cough up her images today of all days, he had been doing very well. He frowned and shook his head, maybe the universe had something big coming his way and wanted him to rid himself of all dark energy. He was not such a superstitious person, this would be something his granny would have said, but he was willing to explore any possibilities and he would hold onto at this time than be lost without anything to believe in a hard and strange world. The perfect American dream, he had found out, was a scam and a mirage. Even most Americans did not live that life. He wondered what must have given them the audacity to believe they could have it.

The cold air intruded into his thoughts and meditations and he looked down, rubbing his hands together. His cup of coffee had grown cold and it was still halfway full. He downed it hurriedly because he hated waste and shivered as the now cold liquid coursed through his body making his insides shiver. He ordered another steaming cup of coffee then to chase away the cold and pulled his coat tighter around his slight frame, waiting to chase the chill away with yet another cup. When the coffee came, he wrapped his hands round the mug and inhaled the delicious aroma of roasted coffee beans that pervaded the atmosphere. His jerky movements in the cold air were arrested by the ringing of his cell phone, he picked it up and frowned, he didn't recognize the number. On the next ring he answered.

"Hello, Mr. Amit Khanna, right?" someone said with a breathless voice talking very fast as if this were a speed talking contest.

"Uhmmm, yes, it is, who…"

"Good, I am Dhiraj from the marketing team of E.B." The man said cutting him off rudely while he plowed on, "we are looking for an automation tester with experience in Java to fill in for a position, and you know Java, right?"

"Yes sir, I have experience with Java" Amit said his heart pounding with excitement. He was overjoyed! He would not have to wait very long before he was placed. That had always been his fear, but apparently, he had impressed the marketers – whose only job was to get the requirements from these job sites and asked the students to customize their resume according to the job description - that they had called on him this early in his training.

"The position is in DC and we need you to prepare for the telephonic interview tomorrow morning, can you do that?"

"Yes sir! I definitely can, thank you sir" the man hung up then without another word. That was considered rude, but Amit was ready to let his uncultured attitude go because he was really grateful for the job placement, if all went well, he would at least have something to contribute to Pooja's engagement.

During a telephonic interview, the Hiring Manager of the company putting out the ads for employees asked questions about the resume, past projects, testing or business analysis process. The training provided by Mr. Sharma and the marketing team had been designed to help students in clearing the telephonic interview. In some cases, if the candidate was weak or had bad communication skills, a stronger candidate took the telephonic interview for him or her. This was a common practice in a lot of Indian consulting firms which went to any extent in order to make the inexperienced hires/ trainees billable.

The interview went well; Amit was asked some questions about the resume the marketing team had sent to the company. He answered their questions confidently and with as much a good grasp of English language as he could muster. The hiring manager also asked him about his knowledge of the software testing and automation skills. They tested his business analysis knowledge and report and by the end of the interview, Amit knew he would get the physical, one on one interview with the MetroTech corporation groups. He did not want to start celebrating prematurely or counting his eggs before they were hatched, but he knew in his gut he would be hearing from them again.

Anand and Sandeep were hearing none of it however. They ordered spicy food from an Indian restaurant they knew in downtown Washington DC and they drank grape juice because Anand was Gujarati and did not drink, and Sandeep had sworn off the heady stuff since getting married.

"It's not every day you get to be chosen and interviewed for a job all of us want and would kill for" Sandeep said lightly, his words colored by a shadow of worry and fear that he might be benched like some candidates from the last batch. This was the fear of every candidate or student who was signed on by E.B. consulting firm. It was still too early to tell whether they would find any company who needed the skill set he possessed and was ready to hire.

"Hear! Hear!!" Anand said in support while opening the bottle of grape juice they had bought and sipping from the bottle while casting a guileless look Amit's way. This man was a brat! Amit laughed loudly, knowing it was for his benefit Anand had licked the top of the bottle of juice. They had dubbed him a germaphobe and health nut all because he took his hygiene seriously. He had once refused to take breakfast one morning because someone had taken a sip from the milk carton and had failed to cap it properly.

"I don't know guys, I think it is too early to celebrate this."

"Nonsense" Anand snorted and refilled his glass while spooning spicy Chicken Karahi and chutneys into his mouth. Amit winced as he accepted the second glass of juice hoping it did not grate on his teeth much later. He always had that reaction to grape juice and its fruit. The curry and chutney were really good though, the taste took him back home and reminded him of his mother's delicious recipe. This was a poor substitute in taste for the wonderful meal they always had during Diwali. The meal was made by cutting up chicken breast and cooking them in peppers and then tossed in the curry and chutney. Amit knew a little about cooking and he had enjoyed it.

"The way you are staring at that food and stalling on every bite, you seem to be talking to a lover." Sandeep punched him lightly on the shoulder, pulling him out of his reminiscing. Amit laughed with them but then, the ache in his chest grew bigger. He missed home, missed his family so much. His sister was going to get married soon and he was going to miss it, his only means of communication with her so far had been through Skype and phone calls that were few and far between. His two brothers were busy trying to make a life for themselves, close to family and love. He wondered why he had ever been considered the smart one, the lucky one who would get to live the dream life, there was nothing dreamy about the life he had here that was for sure. Here he was in a strange place trying to make his way in a World that was not his. He never belonged, never felt like he did anyway. If it had not been for Anand, he would have gone through these past few years alone and chasing a dream he was not sure he still wanted. Now, he had Sandeep too, and they had formed a bond of sorts borne out of mutual interest and goals. He could not help but be grateful for his wonderful friends.

A few days later, Amit got a summons to Dhiraj's office at the marketing department of E.B. He had no idea why, but he could really well guess. Dhiraj was seated in his swivel chair facing the glass windows of his 10th floor office, the view was not much Amit could see, but it was a welcome reprieve from staring at the cluttered desk before him now. Dhiraj turned his chair to face him when he heard the door close behind him his face becoming suddenly animated. The man reminded Amit of an over active 5-year-old who was excited about everything. His movements were always jerky, and he spoke as if he was in a speech race with someone. His hands gesticulating continuously as if they had a mind of his own and right now Amit could see the tic in his left eye as he spoke. The man looked like he was always on a high and Amit tried to imagine waking up tackling life with that kind of energy. It was bound to be exhausting.

"Welcome Mr. Khanna, I'm glad you're here. It seems you made quite an impression on the hiring manager for MetroTech Inc." He smiled at him then, his teeth a snow-white contrast to his brown face. The man also took his dental hygiene seriously too, Amit wondered to himself.

"They want you to come in on Monday for the one on one in-person interview." He stapled his fingers and gave Amit a meaningful glance, "You know what it means right son?" Amit knew what he was trying to say but still it irked him that he had called him 'son', he was maybe in his late 20s and he already had the elderly entitlement mentality.

"Yes sir, I know what it means."

"You have to tweak your resume to meet up with their requests and then you have to memorize all the projects you have supposedly done so that there would not be a mix up or inconsistency somewhere. You have to cram the concepts of software testing and business analysis, do you understand Amit?" he said everything in the same breath and Amit was slightly worried, searching his face for any signs of cyanosis. How could someone hold his breath that long and talk so much at the same time? It must have taken careful practice.

Amit understood what he was saying; their resumes were doctored, with falsified past experiences lettered in to suit the position they were being sent in for. The more skill and education one had, the less doctoring their resumes needed and the easier it was for them to clear the interviews. Amit let him know he understood, and he was going to start in on the cramming right then and excused himself. A part of Amit was excited, but the other part was nervous; what if MetroTech saw through him and his fake resume, he could get in trouble for it.

Monday came soon enough, and Amit headed off to the metro station heading towards the Foggy Bottom metro in DC. He made sure to not soil his really expensive suit lent to him by Dhiraj from marketing. E.B. consulting made provisions to outfit their candidates for the interview when they could not afford a nice outfit. The white shirt Amit wore was a size too big, but he had tucked it in tight into the navy slacks that fit quite well. The navy-blue blazers also fit like it was made with him in mind, it was snug and comfortable, but Amit liked the fact that it somehow made his spine stand straighter and gave his posture a proud stance. While he had prepared this morning, he had looked wistfully at the clothes brushing his hands across the fine woolen fabric and he sighed. It must be nice to be able to afford clothes like this, he had daydreamed about walking into Everard's clothing stores in Georgetown and coming out looking like a GQ model. Soon, Amit promised himself, very soon he would be earning enough to afford the kind of life he wanted.

The train was fast filling up as people were trying to get to their businesses and work on the first weekday morning. Amit was lucky to find a seat before they were all taken. An elderly woman took the seat beside him almost immediately. She smiled at him as she sat down, her face lighting up and the wrinkles that adorned her weathered face smoothed out momentarily. Amit was stopped short; it had been a very long time since any random person had gone out of their way to smile at him. He smiled back and returned her greeting good naturedly, thinking she was really nice. He settled into his seat and closed his eyes to run through the information he had been memorizing all weekend one more time. He had just gotten halfway through when a hand nudged him. He opened his eyes and investigated the earnest face of his elderly neighbor.

"Big day at work dear?" she asked with a sort of southern accent, her voice clear.

"Job interview" he smiled back at her appreciating her friendliness but wishing he could be left alone to run through his lines again.

"Aahh, no wonder you seem nervous child," her voice was pleasantly curious, and she smiled at him sweetly again. "My Billy was so scared his first day at work too, I had to make him chamomile tea. It soothes the nerves." She pulled out a picture from her purse and proceeded to show him a red haired and freckle faced young man in his early thirties that apparently was 'her Billy'. He smiled politely and made a nice comment about her son before turning away again. Poor woman probably was lonely and craved conversation, or she was just a chatty person naturally. Amit wished the circumstances were different and he could really chat, he would have enjoyed her attention. She somewhat reminded him of his granny. She however could not be stopped; she went on to show him more pictures of her Billy and husband, then cute pictures of her grandchildren regaling him with tales of their childhood. Amit listened out of an inbred ability to be polite and he tried to say the appropriate things to her at every pause in her story. Just before he got off the train at Foggy Bottom, she turned to him and pressed a package into his hand still smiling that pleasant smile. "For your nerves son, Chamomile tea,"

"But..." she shook her head at him and thrust the brown bag at him more. "It's ok; I want you to have it. Good luck for your interview son."

He thanked her then took the brown bag which contained a thermos flask and alighted. Her kindness and friendliness were touching, in a country where minding one's business was the norm, anyone who went out of their way to be nice and courteous to others should be cherished. Somehow, Amit knew that this interview would go well, probably because his day had started out like this; with random kindness and luck. His anxiety was momentarily forgotten by the time he got to MetroTech. He had arrived one hour earlier than scheduled, some offices were still closed and the people milling around were quite few. He greeted the African American receptionist and took his seat in the lobby area. The old lady's chamomile tea proved to be as good as she had claimed. The slightly mint taste was really soothing, and it smelled good. The thermos flask was stainless steel and of good quality, and he hoped he would run into her again, so he could return it. Soon, his breath became relaxed and he breathed in deeply. Thanking the universe for the kindness of a strange kind old lady. A couple of hours later, she directed him to a door down a corridor, stating that the Human Relations Officer was ready to see him then. He followed her directions to a door marked HR and knocked, he was asked to come in and sit. The man in the office introduced himself as Denzel Smith and Amit thought his voice sounded familiar. He probably was the guy from the telephonic interview, but Amit was not sure what the man's name had been.

The interview went fast, the questions much the same as the ones asked in the telephonic interview. Mr. Denzel Smith kept twirling his pen when asking Amit, the questions and writing furiously when he started answering.

"That was great Mr. Khanna, we would get back to you soon" Mr. Smith stood up and shook his hand firmly.

"Thank you, Sir." Amit looked at the man closely, trying to gauge his performance from his face. Nothing showed though. He guessed he would find out how he fared later. He hoped though that he had not messed up this opportunity because he had heard that at E.B., the more interviews you flopped, the lesser the chance for you to get placement and it got to a point where you had to pay them the $25,000 they had agreed in the contract because you were considered a liability. All these thoughts ran through Amit's mind as he walked to the elevator barely looking up. He had gotten to the elevator doors before he noticed the ashen face staring at him from the elevator car that was still open. He stopped short when he saw her, he had come out this morning knowing today would hold the unusual and would even be unpredictable. He always had that premonition or the sorts, and it was never wrong. But no premonition would have prepared him for the sight that was greeting him now. Her face was one he would never forget, every line and freckle on that face he knew. Even if she was wearing fancy clothes and she had dyed her hair black and pulled it into a savage back knot. She had lost a little weight since the last time he saw her, and she looked somehow grounded now, no more of the untethered look she had had from their last meeting, but she was still the same.

He stepped into the elevator car then, his eyes still locked onto hers and he smiled slightly. "Hello Lisa."

CHAPTER 7- REUNION

Lisa swallowed hard at the sight of him. She nodded at him lightly and stepped back to let the car accommodate him. "Hello Amit, good to see you." They stood there frozen in time as all the air in the car seemed to have been sucked out. Sweat pooled behind her neck and made the scratchy tweed jacket she was wearing extra prickly. He still looked the same; a messy crop of dark brown hair that always seemed to get into his eyes she had always teased him about his very difficult to tame hair. Even the way he smelled had not changed; sandalwood and old spice, with that clean soap smell and his musk which was all him. She remembered telling him his scent had character and that even if he changed the cologne, it would pretty much remain the same.

Amit barked a laugh suddenly; he probably could not take the oppressive silence any longer. He turned to look at her and her heartbeat sped up, the traitorous organ hammering painfully in her chest.

"I never once imagined that when we would finally meet it would be like this." He said looking straight at her. Her pulse became a steady throb in her throat, she could not for the life of her figure out why she was having this kind of strong reaction to Amit after all that time. Maybe it was because of the way she had treated him back then. Yes, that's what this was; she told herself, it was guilt about the way she had treated him because she was grieving. She was going to tell herself that, but somehow, that theory sounded hollow to her.

"You look good, Amit." She swallowed, kicking herself in the butt mentally for saying something so dumb.

"Seriously?" he looked at her incredulously and then chuckled. "Smart mouth Lisa who always had a comeback for every comment is tongue tied in my presence? I thought I would never see the day!" he said still chuckling. She winced at the sarcasm in his tone.

"What are you doing here?" she tried again, another piss poor effort at making conversation. *What is wrong with you Lisa?* She berated herself in anger, trying to regain her composure in front of him. He laughed outright then and gave her a look like he knew she was making a very poor attempt, but he was going to indulge her. That look was very foreign on Amit's face, at least the Amit she had known, her friend.

"I came for a job interview at MetroTech. Quantitative Analysis and software testing or whatever fancy name they call it, I applied to help crunch numbers." He shrugged, a genuine smile playing at the corners of his mouth and something tugged at Lisa's heart. He still had his self-deprecating humor; her Amit was still there somewhere. Wait, what? Her Amit?!! Get a grip Lisa! She chided herself.

"What are you doing here yourself Lisa?" his tone was kinder.

"I work here." She held her breath, trying to gauge his reaction to the news they would possibly be working together in future. He just nodded, his expression guarded. She acknowledged the fact that this Amit was somehow still the same, but at the same time he was also a little different. His eyes were no longer guileless, and his expressions were no longer there for everyone to see; he was guarding it well, like a man who had known hurt. He hoped it wasn't her who had caused that change in him. He seemed a lot more mature now.

"Well," he smiled then. "It's a good thing I did badly in the interview today." As if on cue, the elevator opened a few floors down and picked up more passengers. Conversation between them ceased and he moved somewhat to the front. Lisa's emotions were all over the place, how could fate do this to her? Amit was here, here! And he would probably be working with her soon enough. She was at a loss at what to do before the elevator doors opened and everyone left, she did not know whether to try talking to him again or let the sleeping dogs lie. When the doors opened, he helped her solve that problem; he left the elevator car without a single glance back at her, swinging his bag and whistling as if nothing had transpired between them just minutes ago. That was when she knew something else about him; Amit Khanna knew how to hold a grudge.

* *

"Is something wrong, Hun?" Matt nuzzled her neck as she tried to make dinner. "Mmmmmmm, whatever you're cooking smells nice," he bit into her neck and inhaled sharply, "You smell nice." he whispered into her ear his hot breath skittering over her back. Lisa clenched her hands over the ladle she was using to scoop soup into a bowl, her teeth clenching in irritation. She berated herself, feeling like crying. Whenever Matt nuzzled her neck and bit into her flesh she was usually reduced to a mass of longing, falling back into his arms. But tonight, she was just irritated by it, she refused to admit it to herself, but her skin was crawling. How could one person buried deep in her past have this much effect on her? Why was Amit's sudden reappearance in her life messing her up so much? It was not like they had anything extra special. She wanted to wail in defeat, but she pulled herself together and away from Matt's embrace.

"Are you sure you are fine?" his face was earnest and slightly worried. She turned away from his gaze and squared her shoulders, making up her mind that she would not tell him about Amit.

"I'm fine, just had a stressful day at work." She turned and gave him what she hoped was a convincing tired smile. He nodded then, smiled and snagged one baby carrot before pulling himself up onto the counter.

"You sure you don't need help?" he asked while munching noisily on his steal. She mustered a slight smile for him then. "Yeah right, as if you really want to help."

"My parent's anniversary party is coming up in two weeks, is that something you would like to go to?" he said while not quite looking at her, he was throwing up peanuts in the air and catching it with his tongue before chewing noisily. Lisa stopped mid motion and looked at him; it must have taken an effort to be nonchalant as he made that announcement. They had been dating for 6 months and been living together for close to four months, this was the first time he had brought up any hints of taking it further or meeting the parents. They had talked about this and she had made sure he knew she was not ready to get married and have kids anytime soon; she wanted to build her career. Knowing Matt, this was his way of trying to test her waters to find out how far she was willing to go now and if her mind had changed any.

"Uhmm, when is it exactly?"

"The 18th of July, Friday night at the family house." He replied giving her a quizzical glance. Did he really believe she would blow him off like that?

"I'll check my schedule and let you know then, otherwise I would love to come." His smile then was blindingly bright. His eyes shone with relief as if extending that invitation was the hardest thing he had to do. "Great then," he said with as much enthusiasm as a five-year-old and her heart warmed. This was what had drawn her to him; his irresistible boyish charm and playful nature. He could make a production out of tasting a new flavor of anything and he was always experimenting with strange things, food, drinks or anything at all. She had teased him continuously about him having a five-year-old trapped in his body.

The first day she had met him; she had just gotten off work and was at her favorite bar with two friends from work. She was just getting started with her second margarita when someone walked up to her;

"You do know your drink choice says a lot about you right?" his eyes were twinkling, and he had a camera slung across his neck, he held the body of the camera in poise as if waiting for permission to start shooting. She had been tired, but she had found him funny and sweet.

"Oh wow, I didn't know I needed a background check before I could get myself a drink anymore." the sarcasm dripping from her voice was tangible, but her eyes danced along with his. They had sustained that conversation till late in the night, her colleagues leaving her behind when they called it a night. He was a photographer and a painter, and he owned a studio in the heart of DC. His first art showing was coming up soon at the National Art Museum.

"So, you're a struggling artist?" she asked him, mock turning her nose up at him.

"I've been told some cougars consider the term stimulating." She had laughed out loud then, not knowing what was so funny, but she knew however that she had a strong urge to laugh around him. He walked her home that night under the stars after taking shots of her and weaseling a promise out of her to pose for him one time. They had seen each other every night since then, and two months in, he decided she should come stay in his condo calling her studio apartment unsafe and not befitting.

She stroked his face now, the food momentarily forgotten, she needed to remember why she was here; she was happy, with someone who made her laugh and live in the moment. He was necessary for her wellbeing and he was the sweetest guy she had ever met. What she didn't know and was too scared to explore was why she felt the need to reinforce these facts. She hoped against hope now as she gave him a lingering kiss that Amit Khanna would not get that job.

****
****

"How was the interview?" Anand asked that night while they lounged in the sitting room. Anand knew him well enough to know something was up with him and it was natural for him to believe that the interview didn't really go well. He forced a smile and looked at them both gratefully, "The interview went well, and the outcome only remains to be seen."

"Then why do you look like you have seen a ghost?" Sandeep was never subtle about the things he said. He was always counted on to not give you bullshit speech (as these Americans often said) or sugarcoat it.

Amit laughed then, at the unlikeliness and strangeness of his day. "I did see a ghost, sort of." He turned to look at Anand, "I saw Lisa today." Anand whistled loudly his eyebrows climbing his forehead and almost meeting his hairline.

"Lisa, as in G-DUB Lisa?"

"Yes silly, that Lisa." He replied looking glum.

"Wait, who is Lisa?" Sandeep looked lost and he had no qualms insinuating himself into a seemingly private conversation.

"The girl who dumped Amit in college, and they were not even dating yet." Anand said with his eyes trained intently on Amit and mischief dancing in them. Sandeep laughed then, not sure he should take Anand seriously. Amit looked at them both shocked and threw file holder lying around at Anand.

Anand dodged the object still laughing and skipped back from the couch. "Seriously man, where did you meet her?"

"She works at MetroTech" he said looking glum.

"Oh shit!" Anand swore. Amit and Sandeep stared at him open mouthed. "What? I can swear too" he said defensively in response to their strange glances. Sandeep smiled and shook his head, "The sheikh also knows how to use cuss words too."

"What are you going to do now Amit?" Anand asked, probably as a ploy to get the attention off himself and onto Amit.

"I guess we'll wait till they get back to me if they do get back to me." He said shrugging. "Wow, you sure don't lack drama in your life that is for sure." Anand said teasing him.

"You are really one to talk Anand," Sandeep said with a laugh. "You with all the ladies in class drooling over and the only one you want, won't even look at you."

Anand groaned and tried to shush Sandeep, the man sometimes had no filter and he talked too much. "What are you guys talking about?" Amit had been so caught up in the job interview in the past week he may have missed important information about his best friend.

"It's nothing Amit, he's just being silly" he waved a hand dismissively in Sandeep's direction which only served to make him laugh harder. Amit would have let it go, but something was different about Anand's face just then. He was blushing!! Anand with the very religious and principled lifestyle who thought women were an expendable extravagance was blushing! Now he was curious.

"It's nothing? And you are blushing this hard?" Amit joined in the teasing, laughing as he probed into Anand's discomfort. "If you don't tell me, I could go ask the ladies." He smiled as Anand shifted uncomfortably in his seat. It was no secret that some of the F4 visa holders and the other ladies in class considered Amit and Anand a good catch and they would gladly tell him anything he wanted to know, especially if it was about his cute friend.

"He has a massive crush on Meghna, the wicked witch." Sandeep offered the information, laughing. Amit gasped dramatically and joined in the mirth.

"Don't call her that, she really is nice." he finished on a whisper.

"Oh my!" Amit laughed disbelievingly. Meghna was a widow, she had come to America to find her husband from an arranged marriage. He had been less than she had expected of him, a drug lord, violent, abusive and involved in many shady businesses. He had been killed barely a few months after she arrived in a gun battle between his gang and a rival gang. She had left everything he owned behind without looking back, now she wanted to get a green card and H1b visa, so she didn't have to go home and face judgmental relatives and in-laws. She however was a grouch, never finding anything funny and trying to infect others with her unhappiness.

"Heck man, why her?" he asked, Anand could very well have any woman he wanted in that class, as a matter of fact, they went out of their way to ensure he noticed them. Why was he torturing himself with this feisty one that would not even give him the time of day?

Anand just shrugged wordlessly as he continued to twiddle his finger. Wow, he was really smitten. Goes to say that you can't help loving who you do love. He of all people knew what that was like, his own heart rate had lost rhythm since this afternoon when he ran into Lisa. Little wonder he had been thinking about her lately, probably the universe's way of warning him. He couldn't help hoping he had passed the interview, he wanted to see her again no matter what all had gone on between them in the past.

As expected, Amit had cleared the interview and was selected for a job as a Software Tester in MetroTech. It was the time called 'Web 2.0 Revolution' and a lot of companies were hiring testers to test the web application and find bugs/defects in their application. Most of the companies were converting their stand-alone applications (applications which were only available if those were installed on your machine) to web-based applications. Amit still had 3 months of Optional Practical Training (OPT) left on his student visa (F-1) and E.B. consulting company's policy was to apply for H-1B if the student had a billable client and had 2 months left in OPT. Amit was right on the cusp and therefore the meeting to discuss H-1B with the HR department of E.B. Consulting was scheduled. These companies had somehow cracked the code of getting H-1Bs approved; they would put an ad out on insignificant newspapers for a week to prove that the company was not able to find qualified candidates for these positions and an H-1B was required. On the visa application the job description was of a Software Engineer with a master's Degree, and it was almost impossible to find a US citizen ready to work as a software engineer for 60,000 USD (especially with 3 to 4 years of work experience) therefore it was easy for these companies to get the visa approved. Also, law firms played an important role in this as they were responsible for the preparation of these applications and provided a rubber stamp. IT Consulting firms and Law firms were making a lot of money by gaming the system and making money off foreign students who got their placements in good companies.

The day he got an email stating the job was his; he got a call from Emily the E.B. Consulting Human Relations Officer who mostly handled the processing of H1b. Amit sort of knew why he was being summoned but he didn't want to be presumptuous about it. He had only ever spoken with Emily twice; one on the phone before he was signed on at E.B. Consulting, and the second time as a briefing before they started their OPT training. He knocked on her door and waited for a few seconds respectfully before letting himself in, he stopped in his tracks when he got in. Bending over Ms. Emily's desk was Mr. Satish Sharma, the CEO of E.B. Consulting. The candidates had never seen the man one on one, he had made a legend of himself and every staff and manager in E.B. consulting talked about him; the boy from Mumbai who had been born into acrid poverty, his father had married several women, so he was one of too many mouths to feed. With sheer determination he had found his way to America and gotten himself an education. He had worked his ass off day and night after school without help from anybody and had built this consulting company from the scratch to solve the problem of young Indian boys who came to America and could not land a job. Now he owned the latest Lamborghini which Amit had heard costed about 300, 000. "You could be like him if you work hard enough" the marketing staff who mostly told the stories always ended with. He had become the success story used to motivate young Indian boys who wanted to achieve their dreams in America.

Mr. Satish straightened up and turned to look at Amit, this galvanized him to action, Amit pulled himself up to his full height and approached the desk his hands trembling.

"Good morning Mr. Sharma, It's an honor to meet you," he extended his trembling hand and then withdrew it immediately as he cleaned it on the sides of his pants to make sure it was not sweaty. He extended it again more hesitantly and Mr. Sharma laughed loudly watching him getting flustered.

"It's ok young man, I don't mind if your hands are sweaty. It's nice to meet you too" he said with a smile, shaking the hand Amit had stretched out to him. "You are Amit Khanna correct? Your reputation sure precedes you" he said to Amit's confused expression. "I believe congratulations are in order, keep it up son, you would soon take my job if you keep up like this." With that he shook his hands once more and took his leave after bidding Emily goodbye. Amit was sure he was star struck, the man had been a little abrupt in his departure, but he didn't mind. It was true he had some issues with the way E.B. Consulting was run but he had to admire the man who had built it. Like it or not, he was living the dream they all wanted, and you had to respect that. He turned to see Ms. Emily watching him with mild amusement, she had been a silent observer to their exchange. He swiftly apologized for being rude, an apology she waved away. "It's okay Amit, everyone has that reaction to him that is why we keep him hidden away. We can't have staff who are walking around with a puppy dog admiration for him all day. It would hurt our productivity." It took a moment for Amit to catch the joke, and he laughed grateful she was trying to put him at ease.

"Well Mr. Khanna," she shifted almost immediately to a more formal stance, steepling her fingers as she looked at him critically. "Do you know why you are here?"

"No ma'am, I don't"

"Hmmmm, very well, pending the employment you have just gotten at MetroTech we want to start processing your H-1B visa. So, I need you to fill these forms and get them back to me in a week's time" she passed over some forms to him in a plastic file jacket. "You do know your first salary would go into the registration and processing of this visa, right?" Amit nodded, he knew the drill; he was required to pay the sum of $6,000 which was close to his salary for 2 months. The fees were to cover the lawyer's fees and the processing fees for his visa. He also had in mind that 30 percent of his salary every other month also went to E.B. consulting for the next 18 months to be able to cover for their training, their accommodation and other expenses the company was incurring..

"Thank you very much maam, I will fill these out before Friday." He nodded at the pile of paper work she had extended towards him.

"Good, keep it up Mr. Khanna, we are very proud of you." She smiled pleasantly at him as she shook his hands before he left. Amit's happiness knew no bounds, right now he was closer to his dream of earning in dollars and making his parents proud in the land of opportunity. At least in a couple months, before Pooja's wedding he could afford her dowry. Maybe not all of it, but a part. He would not be considered dependent anymore, he was closer now to be his own man!

He couldn't wait to share this bit of news with his roommates, but he had to wait, Anand had gone for an interview in a tech company in California and he was coming back in a few days. He skipped as he walked, at least Sandeep would share in his joy. There was one thing that colored his happiness a little though; it was the thought of seeing Lisa again.

CHAPTER 8 – NEW AGE SLAVERY

Amit went through his orientation week at MetroTech uneventfully, he was taken through a crash course on software testing which was tailor made for MetroTech company. He was introduced to all the IT and computer tech guys in an office room where he was assigned a cubicle.

"Please feel at home here," Mr. Kraan the tech department chief said to Amit after the introduction rounds had been gotten out of the way. "These guys are your family now," he gestured to the faces around the room as he addressed Amit in their presence. "You would be spending 8 hours, 6 days a week with these guys and that is 48 hours a week and it is the best productive time of your days. So, I think they qualify for that title of family, don't you think?" he finished on a chuckle. Amit offered a token half-hearted smile in response just to be polite. He looked around the room, about half of the guys- five of them- there were Indians (lending credence to the Indian guys' stereotype), three more were Chinese and a guy that looked so much like Wesley snipes in his crew cut whom Mr. Kraan had introduced as Myles was from Jamaica. Mr. Kraan himself had an accent he could not quite place, but Amit was sure he was either Russian or Peruvian.

The guys took turns standing to shake Amit's hand and welcoming him to the 'fold'. Amit already loved it here in this room. The whole week went away uneventfully, and not once did he ever run into Lisa. He wanted to think they were carefully avoiding each other, but he wondered; had she lied to him that day? She certainly had no reason whatsoever to lie but he had realized in his last days with her in school that he hadn't known her quite well. He didn't want to entertain the possibility of her being this manipulative, but he was happy for the respite all the same.

By the end of that week, he went to Emily's office to submit his H-1B visa processing paperwork. He office door was ajar, and Sandeep was seated in the office with two other guys in their batch. They seemed to be in an intense conversation because she signaled him to wait a little while she finished with them. When they were done, it was Gowan one of the other guys from class who told him in broken and heavily accented English; "She see you now." Sandeep had left without meeting his eyes.

He entered her office a little worried now, she was packing up some documents on her desk and only acknowledged his presence with a nod without looking up. "Sit down Mr. Khanna," he said after a while and then gave him her attention.

"I came to submit the paperwork for the visa processing ma'am. I have filled everything."

"Oh, good! Now I can arrange a meeting with the law firm. You could meet your lawyer next week." She smiled pleasantly. He wanted to be critical of her, shrewd and calculating as she was. He wanted to be mad at everyone in E.B. Consulting, but he was still grateful, he still owed them his employment and half bread was still better than none.

"That conversation you were having with the guys seemed intense," he said a little haltingly referring to the meeting she held earlier with Sandeep and the rest. "Everything ok?"

"Oh, it's nothing you should concern yourself with Mr. Khanna, to get to the top you have to make some really hard decisions and sacrifices." She said and smiled at him.

When he got back to his quarters, Sandeep was parking his stuff and bringing them out to the balcony while Anand watched him with a helpless expression on his face.

"What is going on here?" Amit asked, trepidation crawling into his voice. He turned to Anand, but he shook his head helplessly at him. "Sandeep? Why are you packing your stuff, did you get a job?" Sandeep stopped and looked at him with sorrow in his eyes, "I'm being deported Amit."

"What?!!" Amit gaped at him in shock, "Why on earth would they do that?"

"My F-1 visa expired about 10 months ago, they got me a placement and tried to do a background check before applying for my H-1B, but it seems my stay here is illegal." Amit slumped into a seat, his legs obviously not able to carry the news. He knew all too well the drill with this; when a consulting company signed a candidate on, the condition was that at least they would still have a year window remaining on their student visa (F-1) and that you could get a placement within that period. It made sense now that Sandeep's visa expired almost a year ago, he had finished his master's degree program in computer technology about two years ago and he had tried to get a job on his own for a while before settling for a Desi consulting company. His contract was null and void since it was based on falsehood. Amit could not blame the man for being desperate, they all were. They all wanted to make the life of their dreams in the land of opportunities, which had been on a mission since they came to disabuse them of their grand romantic illusions.

"Can't E.B. consulting do something for you?" Anand spoke up for the first time since Sandeep had walked into the room and announced that he was leaving. "Surely they can come up with another falsehood to cover your tracks if they want to. The whole system is delicately built on fraud and deceit clearly."

Sandeep gave a chuckle, the bitterness in his tone was very clear; "Emily says they can't help me, they don't want to put their company at risk. Apparently, I am very lucky I am not being sent to prison." He gritted his teeth and shook his head and Amit saw the tears gathering in them, he looked away sharply his heart breaking. He had never seen a grown man cry and he really felt bad for him.

"It's kind of a good thing," Sandeep said trying to sound light, at least I get to see my family again." He winced on the words and Amit's heart went out to him, how would he go back and admit to his family that he had failed after trying so hard for 7 years. His dreams had been shattered and there was nothing to look forward to. When he was done packing, he bid them farewell and left with the E.B. Consulting car that would take him to the airport where the authorities were waiting for him.

"Remember *Bhai*, (which meant 'brother')" he said to Anand before he left, "Meghna is all bark, she's a scared dog. Don't give up on her." Anand laughed then, it came out sounding like a sob. He hugged Sandeep tightly.

"I will surely miss you brother," he said to Amit as he enveloped him in a hug. Then he left. As Amit had suspected, the other two guys left with Sandeep that evening. Apparently, he had not been the only one desperate to stay in America.

****
****

Anand stood by the door to Meghna's quarters, his hand frozen mid-way to the door. He wanted to talk to her so bad, but he didn't know how she would react to him today. Her responses had almost always been rude and uninterested, but he was not giving up. Not by a long shot. He knocked on her door and waited, when he heard footsteps approaching his heart slammed harder in his chest, why was he always such a mess around this woman? He tried to wipe the sweat on his forehead quickly before the door was opened and was mostly successful before Sonia's slight frame filled the doorway. Relief washed over him tinged with a touch of disappointment, at least with Sonia, he could buy more time to compose himself. She stared at him with a slightly amused expression, her eyebrows almost meeting her hairline.

"Err…… is Me…Meghna in?" he stuttered like a bumbling fool, and that made Sonia giggle uncontrollably for a few minutes while she tried to cover her mouth with her hands. Anand kicked himself mentally; he just had to make a fool of himself before this slight girl! Of course, he had been the butt of some of their jokes with how clumsy he was around Meghna. It must be an open secret that he was trying to court the hard to get 'witch'.

"I'll go call her for you," she said with a slight shake of her head and she skipped back into the house still giggling like a schoolgirl. A few minutes later, she came back dragging a reluctant Meghna to the door. She stood behind Sonia and would not meet his eyes. Sonia looked from one of them to the other, trying to figure out what her role could be in all of this and maybe how to extricate herself from the sticky situation. When Anand stood there for another few minutes not doing anything like a fool and just staring, Sonia sighed in defeat and stepped away.

"Stop this you two, I'm going inside." She said and subtly pushed Meghna out before closing the door behind her.

"What do you want?" Meghna asked defiantly. She seemed to have recovered her spunk after being momentarily shell shocked. She crossed her arms and turned away from him slightly, and from her body language, Anand knew he was losing her fast.

"I'm leaving for Los Angeles in a few days, I got the job. I guess I just wanted to see you one last time before I go." she turned towards him and Anand was sure he had her attention now. She looked at him with an enigmatic expression, her face giving nothing away.

"Is that all you wanted to say?" she asked him her voice breaking on the words, she cleared her throat once and swallowed hard while still looking at him with one eyebrow spiked up.

"I also wanted to tell you once and for all how I feel about you, if you still don't want to see me I'll go away and never bother you ever again." When she did not say anything to counter his words, he continued; "I love you Meghna, I love the fact that even with everything you've been through, you came out strong. And that does not mean I pity you." He said raising both his hands up as if in defense, he must have seen something in her eyes that must have felt insulted by the prospect of his pity. "I love your strength and determination, and I love how smart you are and how you are not afraid to show it in a World that is supposedly dominated by men. I hoped you would let me get to know you better and take care of you because Meghna, you don't have to be so strong all the time."

She stared at him with a deer in the headlights look for a few minutes, momentarily losing her bravado and usual snotty comebacks. She chuckled then, "How long it must have taken you to memorize that." She shook her head then and stepped forward, her face a mask devoid of emotion. She hugged him, holding on for a few minutes before letting go. "Goodbye Anand, I hope you have the life you deserve." There was a hint of regret in her caramel colored eyes, but her words were like a blow, knocking out the flickering light of hope in his eyes from when she hugged him.

He nodded then, swallowing his defeat and rejection. "Very well then, goodbye." And with that, he left.

Amit was waiting for him when he came back home, he looked at him expectantly; "What?" he asked impatiently, staring him down. He must have seen the way his shoulders were slumped because he said; "She rejected you." It was not a question, and Anand did not need to answer. "Well, looking on the bright side, at least you won't have to battle with a long-distance relationship and you're going to Los Angeles! There's bound to be an overflow of beautiful damsels in distress to rescue."

Anand gave a halfhearted chuckle, grateful to Amit for trying to soften his rejection and lighten the mood. He was going to miss Amit and he told him as much. "I will miss you too friend, I'm the only person you can be in a long-distance relationship with mister."

"Of course," Anand said laughing now, "I'll come to visit you often honey." He slapped Amit's back and went in to finish parking. Tomorrow, they would both be going their separate ways, Amit had also been given an apartment choice from MetroTech in the heart of DC and he was also moving out tomorrow. They were both trying to make their dreams come through and building their chosen careers in the land of opportunities. Tomorrow, they were going to be a step closer to their ultimate dream; a permanent residency card in the United States.

****

Meghna stared through her sitting room window as Anand walked home with his proverbial tail between his legs. The bitter taste of regret colored her tongue and for ne second, she allowed herself to think about what she might have had with Anand if things were different. She wished she could trust him when he said that he loved her, but his words still sounded hollow even with the sincerity in his eyes and his romantic gestures.

"You ran him off again?! Sonia asked from behind her as she tried to see over Meghna's shoulder. Meghna gritted her teeth in irritation; Sonia had a habit of sneaking up on people which she found very annoying. "Why do you always do that, Meghna? This one seems like he genuinely loves you." Her voice was heavy with concern and sadness for her friend. Meghna turned to look at her and shrugged, "It would not have worked out anyway, and he is leaving for Los Angeles tomorrow." She was careful to avoid Sonia's eyes as she said it, or she might see through her lies. The girl had always been very perceptive.

"You know, not every guy you meet is Suresh." Meghna turned to look at her sharply, the indignant fire back in her eyes. "Don't ever mention that name around me, ever again."

Sonia's eyes were deep pools of black and overflowed with sympathy for her. She resented that look and stomped into her room without another word, leaving Sonia to stare after her with her annoyingly knowing eyes.

She slammed her door and fell into her bed in a heap. She curled up in the fetal position and hugged her pillow to herself. She closed her eyes tightly and tried to go back to the time before her life went to ruins, when she was still happy and believed in love;

She and her family had lived in East Delhi, she was the first of five siblings and her father's plans had been to send her to the New Delhi College of Engineering after her high school education, those plans were well underway until her father came home one day saying excitedly that he had found a suitable match for Meghna. Her family had been overjoyed by the possible alliance to a good family who had a son in the United States and no one had ever once asked her what she wanted.

"I always knew you would make us proud *Beta,*" her mother told her with shiny eyes the night before her engagement party as she drew henna on her hands. Meghna remembered the anger and great sadness that had overtaken her, she did not want to be married to someone abroad, she did not even care about marriage right now, and she just wanted to go to engineering college. She told her mom that and her mother gasped as if what she had said was inconceivable and unheard of.

"Come Beta," her mother had said drawing her closer into her embrace, I know how you feel about this, but we can't spit on the kindness of the Guptas, they have accepted this alliance requesting for very little dowry. Surely it is a blessing from Lord Krishna himself. And you can still study engineering in America if you so wish."

"But I don't love him, I don't even know him!" she wailed. Her mother shushed her, looking around nervously. "Quiet child, your father might hear, a daughter's role is to please her father, and after then, to please her husband. And you would learn to love Suresh Gupta, Lord Shiva would make certain of It." her mother had consoled her, and the marriage rights were done in an auspicious time and was supposedly blessed by the gods.

A few weeks later, Suresh's parents had sent her on a plane to Washington DC where Suresh stayed, and her horrors started. He had wanted nothing to do with her, had not wanted a wife at all. She had been a nuisance he loathed. He had also lied to his parents and hers; he was not a professor anywhere, he was a drug lord who ran an underground gang that dealt in everything illegal. He would not hear of her wishes to get an education and he beat her at every slight provocation. As these memories swirled around in Meghna's mind, she rocked herself clutching her pillow to herself as she tried to bury the most painful and most horrifying of them all.

One day she had gone grocery shopping and one of Suresh's men saw her talk briefly with another Indian man at the grocery store and had sent word back to Suresh. When she came back he had beaten her to almost an inch of her life and then proceeded to ravish her when he had never previously ever sought her company before. That night, after raping her; he had then passed her on to his men who had taken turns with her sometimes even twice. She thought she would die, she prayed for it, but morning met her still there, hanging onto a life she now despised. She remembers wishing him death, she had wished and prayed to any God who would listen as she lay curled up on the floor that he would know death. She must have wanted it with all her heart because that day he left with his men at noon and never came back. A few days later, his bullet ridden body was identified and cremated and then sent home for a funeral.

She had not realized she was crying until Sonia came into her room and held her saying soothing words to her. The gut-wrenching sobs that tore out of her stomach seemed foreign to her, she had not known they were coming from her own throat. Her pillow was also soaked, and snot clogged her throat and nostrils, but she could not stop herself. She tried to remind herself she was no more trapped in that past, she was no more a victim of circumstances, and she had risen above it and taken control of her life. She had gotten an education in engineering as she always wanted, now she was on her way to get placement for a job, doing something she absolutely loved doing. She was a survivor and he was dead, he could not hurt her anymore.

Sonia continued to rock her in her embrace till she stopped crying, all the time whispering repeatedly; "It's okay, no one would hurt you now. You are safe." When she stopped, she turned to thank Sonia who waved her gratitude away with a flick of her hands.

"This one really got to you? That's why you had to revisit your past."
Meghna did not answer her, hating the weakness she sometimes
showed with her flashbacks. "I'll be fine she said with an air of
finality, if only her stern voice could convince her heart and not just
her friend. She knew with a certainty that this Anand with the most
sincere and earnest eyes she had ever seen had gotten under her skin
and she would miss him.

****
****

Amit stretched his arms out tight above his head, widening his
legs as he went. He felt really good. The apartment he had moved into
in DC was very close to where Anish –one of the Indian guys in the IT
department in MetroTech and Myles the Jamaican guy lived. Their
shared apartment was just a few blocks down and every morning, they
took runs around the neighborhood. They had been talking about their
work out routine one morning in the office and they had asked Amit if
he would love to come with them. Amit was ecstatic, he didn't have
friends close by and he appreciated the fact that they were extending
their hands of friendship to him.

This morning, they had woken him by 6 am and they started
doing laps around the block. By his second lap, Amit was breathless
and panting like a dog while his friends had not even broken a sweat.
He tried to run another lap, halfway through he felt his lungs would
burst open and he collapsed on the floor. Anish and Myles were good
sports about that, teasing him about not being in shape. "Should I get
you a resuscitation kit?" Myles asked, his eyes sparkling with mischief
and Amit colored with embarrassment. Myles laughed hard then,
enjoying the strong reaction Amit had to being teased.

"Don't sweat it man, it's just your first day working out." Myles said patting his shoulder his eyes taking on a sympathetic quality. "You did fine actually. Take all the rest you want and maybe do some stretches." Amit nodded and with that Myles sprinted away, trying to keep up with Anish. Amit continued to stretch, extending his hips with his arms behind his back. Just as he was getting ready to take another lap and go home to prepare for work, he spotted the last person he wanted to see; Lisa, getting into a car with a man, obviously dressed for work. He stopped and stared, not believing his eyes. It was just his rotten luck that she lived in his neighborhood too. Before the man she was with drove off, she turned, and their eyes met, hers echoing the shock in his own.

Sandeep got off the plane at the Delhi international airport and as he went through baggage claim his heart thudded heavily in his chest. He had been allowed to make a phone call from the holding cell where they had been kept before being put on the plane. He had called Sanjana and amidst his tears of defeat, he had managed to tell her how he had failed her and their kids, had told her he was coming back home in the most shameful way possible.

"It's going to be okay my love," she had said amidst her own tears, "we will meet you at the airport." He was going to say more, but that was all the time he had been given so he had to hang up. Now he was nervous as he was not sure how his family would receive him. He was scared his Bashu would not recognize him and was terrified of facing Sanjana after failing her. He didn't want to think about his parents and relatives, he was sure their reception of him would be bad. He had failed them all after all, and they were even bound to make fun of him. He would be surprised if they even came to the airport to welcome him home.

He had gotten through baggage claim and customs, as he was moving towards the arrivals area, he saw her. She looked a little different, her dark hair was cut shorter than remembered and her hips seemed wider from the birth of two children, but it was still his Sanjana, his sweet and beautiful Sanjana. And she was holding a sign with his name on it while his two children flanked her, Pratik an exact replica of him when he was seven years old. He saw the first time she recognized him, how her cheeks flushed, and she inhaled deeply as if bracing for something. Then her face broke into the most beautiful smile he had ever seen on her yet.

Time seemed to stand still as he got lost in her eyes, drinking in the chocolatey goodness reflected there. She dropped the sign and that seemed to galvanize him, he sprang into motion and got to her in three long strides. He got to his knees when he got close enough and hugged her middle, releasing all the pent-up frustration and disappointment he felt. He apologized repeatedly to her for failing her while she cried and stroked his hair.

"All will be well Sandeep, all will be well. Welcome home." She hadn't said much, but already the shame was lifting. He did not know what it was about this woman that soothed him even when she had not said anything. He encouraged himself in the fact that no matter what he faced here back in India, he would be fine. He had his Sanjana and his children with him. Pratik tugged at his coat sleeve, looking at him with the curiosity seven-year olds were known for.

"Papa?" Pratik asked still staring at him with intense scrutiny. His heart swelled, and he gathered him into his embrace. "Yes Beta, its papa." Bashu stood still, looking a little uncomfortable, but when he stretched out his arms to her, she accepted his hug too. Sanjana joined them in the group hug, laughing with the tears still tracking down her face. Sandeep was happy. Yes, everything was right with his World! What else could he possibly want?

CHAPTER 9 – PACK OF CARDS

Lisa's desk was a mess, the clutter of files and her knickknacks were overwhelming and the paperwork she had to sort through was dizzying but for the life of her, she could not concentrate and work. Not when her distraction was a 5 foot-eight East Asian man with hair the color of coal and eyes like hot chocolate and cream who at one time in her life had been her closest friend. The day she heard he had been employed at MetroTech, she had taken a week off claiming she was sick. She had come back from visiting her mother in Jersey Shore and had come back seemingly prepared to face him and explain what had happened three years ago while they were in school. Since then he had been avoiding her, always making sure they were never in the same space at any given time. He even lived in her and Matt's neighborhood she was positive, she had seen him around several times in the morning working out, but he still was very slippery.

Even though she sort of expected this, it still stung that he would not even acknowledge her presence when she was around him let alone give her the opportunity for a decent conversation. The work stations in the offices on the third floor were faulty and all the IT guys had been running around all morning trying to find the problem and rectify the situation. She had seen Amit amongst them running from the server room to some offices; he had walked past her office several times without so much as a hello or good morning. And this irked her greatly, because whatever she thought Amit was capable of, outright rudeness was not one of them. The Amit she had known would never disrespect an enemy let alone a close friend no matter how they had treated him, but she was beginning to learn now that this Amit was much different from her Amit.

She swore and rose from her desk. If she could not concentrate on her work because of her agitation, she might as well confront the source of all her angst. Maybe put him in a foul mood too. Wasn't there a saying that misery loved company? He was in the server room alone, his back turned towards the door. She closed the door behind her, hoping they had at least some time before another tech nut came into the room.

"You are going to have to acknowledge me one of these days, you know." She said from behind him gently, keeping her distance from him. He whipped around immediately and looked at her, an expression she could not quite read on his face. Soon enough it was gone, replaced by a look of mild irritation and anger.

"What are you doing here, Lisa?" he whispered fiercely coming at her with short, sharp strides.

"Why do you keep treating me like I don't even exist?" he barked a laugh, shaking his head. "I got the sense three years ago that you wanted to be treated that way."

"I didn't know you had picked up pettiness too, it does not look good on you." He swore then and came towards her. "Don't you dare talk to me like that! You don't even know me anymore." The truth of his words cut through her like a knife. It really was true; she didn't know him anymore. The Amit she knew was not petty and did not have this hardness in his eyes. She had been able to read all the expressions on Amit's face, but not anymore. She swallowed then and nodded, "Fair enough, but at least give me time to explain Amit, I can't seem to concentrate on anything anymore with you around. Could we at least clear the air between us? Maybe lunch?"

She tried to reach for him, but he flinched ever so slightly, cutting her deeper where the hurt would never show. "Are you sure your white boyfriend would not mind you having lunch with the smart brown boy?" The words were said gently, but the cruelty and disdain behind them were tangible.

She gasped and looked up at him as though he had struck her, and he sighed. "I'm sorry Lisa; apparently you bring out the worst in me. I will meet you at the coffee shop during break." He touched her shoulders softly and gently guided her out of the room before they were caught by some office busy bodies and reprimanded.

Amit collapsed on the door after he had closed it, exhaling roughly. He could not believe the cruel things that had come out of his mouth just now. He had never talked to anyone like that and he certainly was not this bitter! True, she had hurt him, but he was blowing it out of proportions. He even had no right bringing up her boyfriend and acting like a jealous child because technically, they had not been dating. He had not even told her he loved her. He sighed expressively then, it had taken all of his will power to ignore her the past week. All he had wanted to do was turn and ask her why? Maybe scream it at her and get it over with. Maybe now he would get his answers now.

Tracey's Coffee Shop was usually buzzing with the office crowd at break time. The place was packed when Amit got there at 12 noon, he was worried about them getting a seat, but he saw Lisa was already seated and had saved him a seat in a private booth by the back. She stood when he came in and waved and he was hit as he always had been by her appearance. He didn't know what it was about her appearance that always was like a sucker punch every time he saw her. Some things had not changed no matter the distance, time and hurt between them.

"Hi, she smiled at him shyly, "I wasn't sure you would come."

"I never have given you the impression that I am not a man of my words, have I?"

"I didn't mean it as an insult Amit, I just wanted to make conversation." Her voice sounded defeated now, the fight gone out of her. "I'm sorry." He said on an exhale.

She nodded, looking at him critically. "Let's call a truce please Amit, we were once very good friends and no matter what had happened I still care about you." Her voice was soft and her eyes earnest, he could not refuse her anything when she was like this.

"Fine," he said nodding. "We'll call a truce." He extended his hands to her then and she took it, her smile returning in full force. He looked around then, noticing how packed the place was and how noisy it was getting. The marketing guys were being loud and boisterous, and he was certain they could not hold a serious conversation in such a noisy place.

"Uhmm, do you want to get out of here? Maybe to somewhere quieter?" she smiled again, the radiance of her smile hitting him every single time. "I thought you would never ask."

He pulled her up from her seat and they walked out of the café amidst all the glances from their co-workers which he tried to ignore. They found a steak house little way from their office, about 20 minutes' drive from there and as they had hoped, it was quiet. They ordered and made small talk till the food came. They talked about the weather, the current American economy and old school mates as if they had never been apart. From her, he heard that Brian had joined the army when he left school, going to a military academy instead. Zoya was married to a Hollywood actor and she was pursuing a career on Broadway. He laughed at that bit of information, the idea of Zoya dancing and singing on a stage somehow seemed inconceivable to him. "I always knew she had spunk, that girl." He said in admiration.

"Oh, she was feisty, that's for sure. Her tenacity and strength saved me from a whole lot of self-destruction." She said softly, her eyes obviously someplace else where he could not see. He stretched his hands out and caught hers, "What really happened Lisa, what happened to your father and why did you shut me out?"

She sighed and looked at him, "My father, he was not supposed to be in the west tower when it went up in flames. He had already come down, but he had gotten a phone call by his friend, the one he had gone to meet to come back and pick up some paperwork from the reception of the firm he had gone to see and, on his way, up again, everything went to shit. We did not even have a body to bury, just some ash in an urn my mother had gone to gather." Her voice broke on a sob and she swallowed reflexively, willing herself not to cry. He tightened his hands on her own, trying to offer her comfort wordlessly.

"I'm sorry." She sniffed somewhat embarrassed by her show of weakness.

"There's nothing to be sorry for, Lisa. You lost someone important to you; that was bound to be hard." She nodded, looking at him with gratitude. "You will be sorry though if you leave this place with gravy still on your jaw." His laughter rang out clear as he wiped the offending sauce off her chin and her breath caught; it was just like no time had passed at all between them, like old times.

'I'm sorry I said all those hurtful things to you back then Amit, you must know I never meant any of them." She said with urgency, holding onto his hand.

"I know you did not mean them at the time, they didn't hurt me. What I could not figure out was why you froze me out for three years. I was your friend Lisa, I reached out to you several times."

"I'm sorry, I was in a bad place for so long" she said swallowing.

"For three years?" much as he tried, he could not get the hurt out of his voice. He hated sounding like a wounded child, but the truth had to be said, he wanted so badly to clear the air between them.

"At first, I was too wrapped up in the grief, the horror of working as a stripper and everything and I took it out on the people that mattered to me, people like you. Later I was too ashamed to come apologize. Those were not the proudest moments of my life Amit, I'm terribly sorry."

He nodded, seeming to have accepted her apologies. "I guess I could have tried harder to reach you if I wanted. But I guess I was scared." She looked at him quizzically, "Why would you be scared of talking to me Amit?"

He looked at her in mock disbelief, "Are you kidding right now Lisa? You were pretty scary then after the attack. With your scary gothic look and those piercings, those must have really hurt!" she laughed covering her face with her hands. "I was NOT scary! I was hurting, and it was a stupid phase I went through. If it had not been for Zoya, I would not have snapped out of it. And yes…. Those piercings were painful as hell."

"I understand perfectly now," he tried to reassure her, "I just wish I had my study partner, it would have made those three years worthwhile."

"So, when did you get a job with MetroTech?" he asked, trying to get off the stickier, serious subjects.

"About a year ago, I had interned there two years ago, and they had promised me a spot on the staff space when the openings came out if I was interested."

"Oh wow, so you were a sort of legacy huh? Must be nice."

"Not exactly a legacy, I was just really good at taking orders and bringing them coffee."

"Is that modesty I hear in your tone Lisa Morgan? I did not think I would see the day!"

"Brat!" she threw her used napkin at him laughing. He caught it easily and started folding it into neat squares while looking at her intently counting in his head till she flinched. He laughed, it had been a habit he had picked up that used to gross her out. She hated him touching soiled napkins and he annoyed her further by rubbing his seemingly filthy hands on her body much later. It seemed a lot had not changed.

"Ewww, you still have that nasty habit. That napkin is disposable and probably has my spit on it." He only looked at her with a triumphant smirk, not saying anything. He stared her down till she gave in and looked away. "Whatever weirdo, just don't touch me with those hands."

"So, what about you Amit?" she smiled, seeming to want to draw the attention away from herself and put it upon him. "What have you been doing since we got out of school?" he chuckled and shrugged.

"Nothing much, my life hasn't been as exciting as yours has been apparently." He went on to tell her about the problems he had encountered getting hired and how he had gotten involved with E.B. Consulting. He explained the process to her sparing a lot of details, enough to make it seem mysterious.

"You know, I actually thought you would be working at owning your own restaurant business by now. With the way you were fascinated by food and its preparation in several hotels and all. I never pegged you for a guy who would end up working in IT and for a company like MetroTech."

"Oh, I still love restaurants and food, if that's what you're asking." He laughed. "I might still pursue that dream, but right now I need to build my career. I do love being a nerd too" she shook her head at him, laughing.

"Well you did have a word to say about everything we had been served in any restaurant. You mind critiquing this one?" she spread her hands out to the chicken and steak they just had.

"Hmmmm, he studied their almost empty plates as if in deep thought, "Steak should best be prepared by first generation immigrants in America or by natives generally. They tend to capture that feeling of home in the very first bite." He smirked at her. "I'm sure these guys are probably very good, but it lacks that special taste from home or real traditional restaurants."

"Oh wow! That was a lot from just one steak." She laughed. He turned up his nose as he looked at the décor, "This place kind of also needs a different décor. You would think the food was boring from the way it has been distastefully decorated."

"Well Amit, if you ever want to open that restaurant let me know. You seriously are missing your calling." He waved it off with a laugh.

They moved on to other topics of discussion, till it was time to get back to the office. They rode the elevator to their stop without any other passenger in tow and as they reached their stop Amit suddenly pulled her into his arms and covered her lips with his own. Her lips tasted like cherries and he swallowed the gasp that escaped from her mouth into his own. He pressed her into the wall of steel and wrapped his hands round her waist while he bit her lips lightly. Her taste was heady and he almost lost control of himself. He almost lost himself in her. He coaxed her lips open with soft bites and snaked his tongue into her mouth challenging her tongue to a tango that was dizzying and intoxicating. He withdrew at the last minute, looking deeply into her eyes. "I've always wanted to do that" he said softly to her, caressing her swollen lips while her dazed eyes got lost in his. Just then, the doors opened, and they were no longer alone together. He smiled at her slightly and left, loving the dazed look in her eyes as she went back to her office. Amit was sure of one thing; he would not be the only one thinking about her tonight. She would be right there along with him, even if only for one night.

Lisa got home that day still distracted, she touched her lips several times trying to relive the feel of Amit's lips on hers. She could not believe her body had reacted so strongly to him, pent up emotions maybe or an attraction that had not been explored then. He had been very gentle yet assertive, coaxing her lips open softly and then dueling her tongue roughly. It was a wonder she had not dissolved into a puddle at his feet. She let herself into the house and found Matt sitting on the sofa all dressed up and with flowers in his hands. He looked up when she came in and managed a half smile which was basically him stretching his lips wide. It did not reach his eyes. "You are late Lis" he said trying to be upbeat about it. Apparently, whatever he was talking about was a big deal for him, but he did not want it to show.

She looked at him funny, "Is there an occasion honey?" he turned to look at her as if she had struck him across the face. "You forgot?"

She tried hard to recall if there was anything she was supposed to remember that was really important; it was not his birthday this month, of that she was sure, he did not have an art showing any time soon and it was not their anniversary. She wracked her head some more and came up with nothing. "I am sorry Matt, but whatever it is must have skipped my mind."

He nodded as if coming to a certain unknown decision in his head. "Its fine, I guess I would go for my folks' wedding anniversary alone." Just then it clicked; the anniversary!! Guilt flooded her chest. "Matt I'm so sorry! I totally forgot!" she tried to touch him but the expression on his face was distant and abhorrent, like he was not there with her in the room anymore.

"Babe," she whispered as she came closer, her hands extended towards him and just shot of touching him. "I'm sorry, I'll go change and meet you out here in a few minutes." He just nodded at her then, his position on the couch not changing at all. She rushed into her closet all the time berating herself for being so preoccupied with Amit. How could she have forgotten this? She was not ready to explore the obvious reasons; that she did not want to go in the first place, that she was not ready to take things further than they were and the most glaring one; that he was not as important to her as she thought he was. She wanted to cry out that it was not true, but the facts did speak for themselves. She dressed up, pushing all those thoughts out of her mind and went out to meet him. He looked up when she came in and stood up to hold her shoulders. "Do you want this, Lisa? Do you think we are moving too fast?" The look in his eyes was tender and pleading at the same time.

She sighed and smiled at him, "Of course I want this, and I'm exactly where I want to be." As she uttered the words, an image of Amit smiling at her after kissing her in the elevator flashed through her mind. Yes, she was lying, but by God she would fake it till she believed she wanted this meeting as much as this very sweet man before her. She would make sure that this would be memorable for him and his folks as they deserved nothing less.

****

On mornings like this cold one, Amit would have loved to sleep in and call in sick. He could not conceive how people coped with this unbearable winter mornings and he was of the opinion that on cold days like this, people who worked hard should be given holidays. The day he had shared that notion with his colleagues, his tech family at MetroTech, had burst out laughing. It seemed like a rowdy bar in there for a few minutes till they had been cautioned.

"You seem to forget the unwritten laws of the American corporate world man." Myles pointed at him laughing. Amit shrugged at him, not feeling the need for a comeback.

That morning however, Amit had stretched and gotten up feeling drowsy. He did not understand why he felt strange today, it was like a premonition and he could not quite shake it. He went for a run as he had been doing with Anish and Myles; they had continued to work out together with Myles helping him to buff up and stay fit. They had hit the gyms on particular days and now, six months into living here, Amit was not so skinny anymore. Today though, he didn't feel like working out with them at the fitness center down the block, he just took a run. However fast he ran though, he could not quite outrun the bad feeling in the pit of his stomach. He stopped to rest for a while, his heart racing. He made a point to call his family because he could not figure out what else could make him so restless; he had a good relationship with his coworkers and he was doing well in the IT department, the last time he spoke to Emily form E.B. Consulting, his visa was being processed and he had even spoken to the lawyer that had been assigned to process his visa so everything was fine he thought. He got back to his apartment and the phone was ringing, he got to the phone still wiping the sweat from his brow with a towel.

"*Beta*…" the voice stopped him instantly, sending slivers of alarm down his spine. It was his mother, and her voice was tear- laden. She tried to speak again but broke down crying now. The sobs tearing through her throat and travelling all those hundred thousands of miles to come rip through his heart.

"Ma, he said softly his heart beating out of his chest. "What's wrong Ma? Is Granny ok?" his heart beat fast, *please god, not granny* he cried in his heart.

"Amit granny is okay, his mom said when she could catch her breath. "It's your …..Your father Amit" she broke down again, her sobs getting louder.

Amit felt cold, his heart rate slowed almost immediately, and time seemed to stand still. He looked around and felt like he was falling through space. He stepped away from the phone, staring at the receiver in his hands as if it were the enemy or the offender. It could not be! His father could not be hurt. There must be a reasonable explanation; he told himself, he would find out. "Mom," he called again into the receiver while he listened to her sniffles and tried to compose himself, so he could be strong for her.

"Mom, what happened to Papa? How bad is he hurt?"

"Oh Amit, if only, he died in a motor accident on his way back from Delhi." Her weeping resumed. Amit inhaled sharply, holding his middle and trying to breathe. His chest was clogged up and his heart hurt so badly. He heard guttural sounds coming from the phone, but he could not muster the words with which to console his mother. "Beta, can you come home? Its urgent and we need you here for your father's funeral, it would have been really important to him." her voice was clear, and he tasted salty water, which was when Amit realized the guttural crying sounds he had been hearing were actually coming from him. Her words sent chills down his spine, he had submitted his passport to Emily for his visa processing and the lawyer had called him a few days ago to ask for some pertinent details and had reassured him his visa was in process.

"Yes Ma, I will try." He said shakily and hung up. The words had left his mouth out of desperation; he could not possibly have told her he may not be able to make it when she was so burdened already. He called Emily's office, his motions mechanical and forced. Papa was dead. His father was gone, he would not see him alive anymore and he had not been able to prove to him he was a worthy son, the tears clouded his vision as he spoke tightly to Emily, making an appointment to come see her this morning. He called in for a leave of absence at MetroTech, just telling Mr. Kraan, the head of IT that he had a family emergency.

"Take all the time you want son," he had said his voice tight, Amit did not need to be told his people like him were a dime a dozen and he had about a hundred people right now who were eager to take his position, but at this point, he could not help the predicament he was in. His family needed him and Mr. Kraan could wait another couple of days if need be.

He got to E.B. Consulting about an hour later, the train had been half filled at the metro station which was fine by him, and he needed the peace and quiet that could afford him. He went straight to Emily's office, nodding at a few marketing guys he recognized and some of his fellow trainees who had probably not been placed. Her door was slightly ajar, but he knocked to be polite. He could see her from the opened crack of the door and she was pacing the length of her office view, mumbling something to herself. She turned around at the sound of his knocking and a tight smile masked her worried face. She was probably stressed, and knowing how Emily loved perfection, she would obsess over it till she thought it was perfect. She waved him in and sat down gracefully. That was one thing about her that always puzzled Amit, no matter how agitated she was, she had her cool and calm façade waiting ready like a cloak and she pulled it on immediately, looking elegant at once.

"How can I help you, Amit, you sounded really urgent on the phone?" Her voice was smooth as molasses, and Amit hoped he could achieve as much calm as this right then.

"I need my passport back, I want to travel home briefly for a family emergency." Her face twitched ever so slightly as he talked. Then she exhaled loudly.

"Do you really know what you are asking Amit? Your visa is under processing for about another six to eight months and you cannot possibly have access to it now."

"I know all that Miss Emily, but I really need to go back home. I just lost my father, I'm his son and I need to go perform his funeral rites." He said his voice rising ever so slightly with every word. "Please Miss, help me." He was begging now, his eyes clouding with tears as he leaned forward, grabbing onto the edges of her desk.

She sighed as if world weary, like he was asking the moon of her. "Look Mr. Khanna, I am deeply sorry about your father. I would really love to help you go see him, but look around you! Do you know how lucky you have been? Do you know how many people would kill to be in your position?" she paused probably for effect and looked at him pointedly before she continued; "Amit, you could be deported, that's what you might be facing if your visa is not processed on time. Your F-1 visa has already almost run out of time, how would you come back if you leave now?"

"Don't you get it?" Amit almost screamed at her, "My father is dead, I need to be with my family! Please Miss Emily, can we not work something out?"

She stared at him visibly unmoved by his plea. "I really am sorry Mr. Khanna, but the only other way would be to fulfill the non-compete contract." Her eyes were matter of fact. He squinted at her, trying to understand what she meant and just then a clod chill enveloped him. The non-compete contract, of course! Anger and desperation coursed through him as he stared at her in unbelief. Every candidate at E.B. Consulting had signed a non-compete contract in case they wanted to leave E.B. Consulting or switch over to another company, they had to pay the company twenty-five thousand USD ($25000). And right now, he did not have that money! He was paying them 30% of his salary already and he barely had enough saved up to cover this trip.

"I don't have that amount of money anywhere! Plus, it's not like I'm leaving E.B. Consulting or anything. I am coming back."

"Well those are the rules Mr. Khanna." She shrugged almost looking bored. A great sense of helplessness and despair swamped Amit, he tried to make sense of his predicament. Basically, he was a prisoner, held against his will in a country he had come to in search of a better life. He left her office without another word, deciding to take a longer route and walk to clear his head. He got home a few hours later, to make the hardest phone call of his life.

When he told his mom, he would not be able to come home, it shattered her; she broke down crying on the phone again. It took willpower he could barely muster not to join her in the crying jag, he cut the call after promising to call back later and went to sleep. He laid down, the weight heavy on him, he had always thought of depression as a hypothetical situation, but now he knew it was real. He wanted to curl up into himself and die, his insides were hurting. He could not sleep the whole night thinking about his father giving him instructions on how to ride the bicycle for the first time followed by the image of him being carried away on the wings of oblivion.

CHAPTER 10 – MARKET COMES CRASHING DOWN

Amit woke up to a pounding in his head that was unforgiving and unbearable; he could only manage to open his eyes to slits while cradling his head in his arms. He massaged his temples and his arm muscles screamed in protest. He had slept in a curled-up position and apparently, he had been asleep for a long time his muscles were sore. It was dark out and Amit could barely make out the clock over his bedpost that said 9:00pm. He groaned pitifully, the only other time he had felt like this had been the day he had gone out to drink with Manoj, Brian and Min Ho in freshman year at G-DUB. He had sworn off alcohol since then, he figured crying could also give you a hangover. The pounding started again like a vibration through his head that swept through the house too. He realized then it was not in his head it was coming from, it was his front door buzzer. Someone was at his door. Amit had no intentions of entertaining visitors today and he figured he would dismiss whoever it was. He padded to the door his best guess being that maybe Myles and some guys from the IT Department had come to know how he was doing. Knowing how rowdy they could be he hoped they did not stay too long.

He opened the door and met the most unlikely sight; he could not have guessed that she would come here, to his house. Lisa smiled at him a little uneasily and waved, "Hi Amit. I heard you were not feeling too well." her smile was shy and tentative like she was not sure she should be here. He and Lisa had lived in the same neighborhood for the six months he had been here and not once had she dropped by. They had developed an unwritten code of sorts since that day in the elevator when he had kissed her. They never brought it up and only ever discussed mundane stuff. They had a good working relationship, but every time they had a conversation, she kept bringing up her boyfriend Matt, even a blind man could have read her vibes, so Amit took the hint and they had stayed platonic.

She gave an awkward laugh and motioned to the door he was clearly blocking, "Aren't you going to invite me in?"

"Oh damn, I'm sorry, come in" he kicked himself mentally; he had probably been gawking at her the whole time. No wonder she had been uneasy.

"You have a nice place here Amit,' she said turning around in his living room to take it all in. he shrugged not having the strength to be modest or anything at all. She turned then to look at him, worry clouding her beautiful blue eyes. "Are you ok? I heard you called in sick." He sighed then, drinking in the sight of her beautiful face marred with worry lines for him. The tears started gathering again in the corner of his eyes and he took a deep breath willing them away.

He squared his shoulders, taking in a deep breath and hated the way his voice shook when he said; "My father is dead."

"Oh Amit," her voice broke on his name, her face a wreath of concern. She reached for him and he let her. She hugged him, clinging to his neck while she buried her face in his chest. "I'm so sorry." She whispered into his chest, her hot breath caressing his flesh and spreading goose bumps all over his body. "How did he die?" she asked him, looking up.

"Car accident, I can't go home to see him now because I don't have access to my passport." He went on to tell her his ordeal with E.B. Consulting and how they had asked for that huge sum of money to give him his passport. He told her too in a flat tone of voice devoid of inflection and how he might face deportation or be denied entry if he left the country without his H-1B visa. "My father would have wanted his son to light the pyre at his funeral" he said, the tears crawling back into his voice. "I really wanted him to be proud of me, of my achievements. They worked really hard to get me here, now he would not even be here to see what I made of myself. I can't even be there for my family when they need me." His voice broke on the last words, his veneer of control cracking as he gave in to the pain he felt. He crumpled to the floor, taking her down with him as he cried his pain away. She hugged him close, cradling his head like a child's as he rocked himself back and forth. She kissed his head, whispering "it's ok" to him.

They stayed that way for a long time till his sobs turned to sniffles and then dried out. She kept cradling his head in her hands even after he had stopped crying, saying soothing words he could not quite hear to him. In retrospect, Amit could not quite say when the mood changed or when the air around them got charged up with sexual energy. But he knew that one minute she was still caressing his head, the next he was looking into the deep pool of her turquoise blue eyes, he could not have been able to resist staring at her luscious pink lips if he had even wanted to try, but he had not even tried. She stared back at him, her breath caressing his face as he traced his fingers across her lips Amit caressed her lower lips, inhaling her scent, drinking her in. he inhaled sharply when she bit his finger and then he sighed and pulled her close. Their lips met slowly, she inhaling sharply as they did. Her hands found their way around his neck and into his hair, she sighed his name and opened her mouth to grant entrance to his tongue. He pulled her closer to himself a little roughly and she moaned, following his hands like a puppet. He lay on the floor and pulled her on top of his body, molding her frame tightly to his. She moaned into his mouth and the heat spread from his mouth down through his insides to his groin. He felt the tightness there, she must have felt it too because she ground into him.

He stopped her suddenly looking deep into her eyes, "do you really want this?"

She nodded eagerly, her eyes deepening to a cobalt blue, the lust making her eyelids heavy and drooping. She tried to control her breathing as she said; "I have always wanted to do this with you."

"What about Matt?" he searched her eyes earnestly, a slight frown marring his brow. She smiled slightly, smoothing out the frown from his fore head. Then without another word she lowered her head onto his in another passionate kiss. He groaned as she ground her hips into his and he pulled her closer, humping her pelvis in an erotic dance. Their coming together was sweet, slow, sensuous and just…..right. He loved her like he had wanted to for a long time, all the years of his silent adoration went into their lovemaking. He caressed her body like it was a temple and adored her with a reverence befitting a goddess. He kept calling her *Pari* which meant fairy, his favorite name for her back in the school. When she cried out her release, it was followed by a jerking so violent it rocked him too. He screamed his own satisfaction a little after her, climbing down the high with a sigh as he kissed her face all over reverently.

He stared at her tenderly as she lay beside him, her body languid and limbs fluid. She purred like a satisfied cat and his heart swelled inside his chest, so much so he thought it would burst out of his body, leaving an empty shell in his thoracic cavity. He traced his thumb and forefinger across her face and feathered light butterfly kisses along the path his fingers were making.

The ringing of the phone roused them both from their lethargic slumber, Amit picked up the receiver expecting a random salesman or maybe even Myles and Anish calling to check in. when he heard the operator asking him to approve the collect call from Mumbai India, his heart started racing again. He approved it and said a tentative 'hello'.

"You as good as spat on his grave you know?!" the voice on the other end of the line screamed at him. He would recognize Pooja's voice over ten thousand miles and with the pain laced through it. He drew in a fortifying breath, "Pooja, I wish I could do anything." He swallowed as he turned his back to Lisa, the moment and the conversation was too private to share with her.

Pooja laughed, the sound mocking and choking with emotions, "He always bragged about you to his friends, you know? His perfect son who had gone to America to make us proud, he did not waste any opportunity in telling anyone who cared to listen that you were following in his footsteps, that you would be the best computer scientist in all of Mumbai." Now he could barely make out her words because of the sobs that wracked through her, she was hiccupping with the force of it. Amit kept sobbing softly.

"Your family needs you now Amit, Ma needs you now.... I need you!" her voice had taken on a pleading quality and she was sniveling too as she pleaded with him to come home. "He would have wanted you to be here, to honor him, to give me away...*Bhaiya.*"

"You know I would move the universe to be with you all now Pooj, but I can't." he cleared his throat which was thick with unshed tears. "Apparently I am now a prisoner of my own ambitions." He whispered to her, his heart breaking along with his voice. "Please be strong for mom and granny Pooj, I love you." He hung up before she could say anything else and break his heart to tiny pieces.

He felt Lisa's hands on his shoulders and almost jumped at her touch, he had all but forgotten she was in the room with him. He kept his back turned to her and kept holding onto the phone receiver as if a piece of home was still there. He felt her massage his shoulders and realized it was not just his hands that were trembling. His shoulders were heaving too, and his lips were quivering from the effort of keeping the tears at bay. The worst feeling Amit decided was not that of defeat and helplessness, it was the thought of disappointing everyone he held dear to him.

"I have let them all down."

"Shhh, don't say that. It was not your fault." She tried to soothe him, drawing his back into a hug.

He spent the night cradled in Lisa's arms, drawing and receiving comfort from her, he refused to think about the moral implications of their actions; he just wanted for once to not bother about responsibilities and the right thing to do, for tonight he wanted to be selfish. He woke up to an empty bed and a note on his bed table. She had left in the early hours of the morning in the classic walk of shame style. He refused to think about the indication of that action, yesterday still seemed surreal to him. Her note read; 'have to go home and prep for work, see you later? Ps: I had a good time.' He imagined her wearing the scent of their lovemaking all the way home that early morning and he found he liked that thought. His father had once told him, that if things got very bad, it had the choice to only get better. So Amit figured since he had hit rock bottom, things would only get better then. How wrong he was.

****

The next week, a wave of upsetting and interesting news swept through the country and it meant a lot for the Indian immigrants living in the United States. The President George W. Bush enacted a law called the H1-b Visa Reform Act, 2004 which would become part of the Consolidations Appropriation Act 2005 and was predicted to succeed previous legislations. The law was an infringement on H1-b visa and an increase of the tax for companies whose hired workforce was H1-B visa holders.

Amit was still trying to figure out what this would mean for him and his future in MetroTech when he was summoned to the office of the Human Relations Officer, Mr. Denzel Smith –the man who had interviewed him for this position. The guys in the IT room had been discussing the current impediment on the H1b visa, everyone almost too scared to explore what it meant for them. They could not help the ripple of relief that went through them when Mr. Smith had sent for Amit.

The man was on the phone talking furiously to someone at the other end. He seemed to be exasperated by the conversation and he slid his hands roughly through his perfectly slicked back hair causing some of it to spring up in the front. The man seemed to remember his hair was slicked back after running his hands through it and he tried to slick it back down in a way that was not so obvious but it only made the hair spring up further. That tuft of hair almost made Amit laugh but he controlled himself. He concentrated on that tiny visible flaw and braced himself up for whatever he would be told by Mr. Smith. He felt somehow like he would better bear the news if he reminded himself the man was not as perfect as he wanted people to believe.

When he was done with the phone call, he turned to Amit with a smile. "Mr. Khanna! How have you been?"

"Fine sir, I have been well, thank you." The man nodded at Amit in acknowledgement. "I hope you have had a good work experience here with us?"

"Yes sir, absolutely."

"You have heard about the current law on H1-b Visas yes?" he asked going straight to the point. Amit nodded, bracing himself up sensing where this conversation was going to lead to. He hoped this law would not impede the processing of his own visa which was almost done.

"My H1-b visa is almost ready sir; he tried to assure the man before he continued. Because hopefully if his visa was ready, then they would not have a problem here.

Mr. Denzel Smith shook his head lightly as he looked at Amit sympathetically. "We do not have an issue with the issuance time of your visa, Mr. Khanna. As you know, the taxes have been increased by about 50% on companies who have H1-b Visa holders as part of their workforce, hereby affecting our revenue and general productivity." He looked at Amit intently to find out how much he had taken in before he continued. "In other words, we can't afford to have all of you all here at MetroTech. We have to let some of you go Amit, we have to let you go."

Amit exhaled as if punched, he collapsed his stiff upright position and fell back into the chair. He was a hard worker, his superiors all had nothing but praise to sing of him, he was a good team player, why would it have to be him being let go? "Uhmm sir," he cleared his throat and sat up, "Why me?"

Denzel Smith shook his head slightly and grimaced as if the question had caused him physical pain. "There was no special parameter used to decide who would be let go Amit. I am sure you have been diligent with your work and you work very hard. But as the last person we hired on, it made sense to the board that it would be you. I am really sorry Mr. Khanna."

Amit nodded absent mindedly as he looked at the man blankly, how wrong he had been that things would now get better. He had not known it would get worse than that.

"............. Mr. Khanna?" he looked up sharply, pulled roughly away from his train of thoughts and nodded not bothering to fully catch what was being said. "You will collect your severance package from my secretary Ms. Wanda on your way out and good luck Mr. Khanna."

He got up then without another word and left, in the outer office Ms. Wanda who apparently had known about the termination of his appointment stood with a sympathetic smile and handed him a thick creamy envelope and a bow to pack his stuff on his way out. He took it hurriedly from her not wanting to be exposed to her unwanted sympathy and left without a word. He was halfway out the door when he realized that he might have been rude to her, but he could not go back then. He got back to the IT room to meet the long faces of his colleagues who must have heard in his absence. News he knew, traveled very fast in a corporate environment like their own. Amit had learnt not to underestimate office gossip and its power. He tried a weak smile as he dumped the package on his office desk.

"Screw the H1-b Visa Reform Act! Anish said so vehemently it made Amit laugh. Anish was an otherwise very quiet person and they had not heard him use inappropriate words before let alone swear. Amit was touched by his strong reaction. "I will miss you too man." He said patting him on the shoulder.

"Hey, y'all stop behaving as if this is goodbye. Amit still lives around the corner." Myles pointed out, trying to lighten the mood in the room. Amit smiled his gratitude and thanked them as he packed up his baggage and left with a final goodbye to the family he had come to know for that short time.

****

"What will you do now?" Lisa asked him when she came visiting the next day. She was leaning on his kitchen counter as he made the dough for some kati rolls he was making for dinner. That was the first time he had spoken to her since their time last week. He was confused by her and he was finding it difficult to figure her out. He had felt that she was avoiding him after she left his place because they had not found an opportunity whatsoever to talk. He figured she was wracked with guilt for cheating on her boyfriend but here she was, acting as if nothing had happened between them.

He shrugged indifferently as he looked at her, "I will go find another job I guess, after I get my visa and passport from E.B. Consulting."

"Have you thought about opening that restaurant Amit? You would be really good at it." She prompted him.

He shrugged again, "I have not given it much thought; besides I love crunching numbers too."

"Think about it would you?" she asked as she absently popped a carrot into her mouth. When he had gotten the dough smooth enough, he wrapped it up and turned fully to face her. "What I really want to talk about now is thus back and forth between us Lisa."

She stopped in her motions and looked at him blankly before her eyes clouded with an emotion Amit was not sure he could interpret. "Amit…. it's complicated…" she tried, flustered.

"It really is not Lisa, or please simplify it for me." He held her stormy gaze with his very calm one.

"I….."

"You are cheating on him" her eyes took on a haunted quality. "Don't say it like that!" she looked like she might cry when he said that, her face looked stricken and ashen.

"How else can it be said Lisa? Do you love him?" he asked then his voice probing yet dreading what her answer would be.

"I do love him Amit….it's just…"

"It's just that you don't love me?"

"Amit…."

"Answer the question, Lisa." He stepped closer to her now slowly, his eyes burning with unanswered questions.

"You have never told me you loved me, Amit." Her voice was barely above a whisper and the tears were already gathering in her eyes.

Amit raised his brows at her and then clucked his tongue, "Is that the problem Lisa? You're still with him because you're not sure I love you?" his voice echoed his doubt.

"Because I do love you Lisa, I have loved you since the first day I saw you. Anyone could see that, except you apparently."

"That is not fair! You never said anything."

"Forgive me if I didn't say anything, the day I would have you pushed me away." She covered her face with her hands, her chest heaving with tamped down emotions. His resolve broke then, and he went to her, taking her in his arms, he held her face between the palms of his hands and caressed her damp cheeks with his thumb.

"Do you love me? I need to know Lisa."

"I do love you, but I can't do this. It does not feel right." Her eyes pleaded with his to understand.

"Being with you feels right! Kissing you, holding you feels right Lisa. Help me understand."

She broke away from his embrace and turned her back to him, "I can't do this, and I need to think."

He swallowed his rejection painfully and let her go. "Well when you are done thinking, you know where to find me. Apparently, I'm not good enough for you." He knew it was cruel to say that last bit, but he could not resist lashing back at her for the hurt he was feeling right then. She groaned and without another sound, she left his apartment and probably walked out of his life as well.

****

"We are sorry Mr. Khanna, there really is no opening for H1-B visa holders here. We will get back to you surely if we find something." The staff manager smiled at him apologetically and shook his hand. It was another tech company and another rejection. He smiled, thanked him and left. As he trudged the streets, he tried not to feel so beat down. Since the enactment of the H1-B Visa Reform Act, it seemed like every company slammed their doors in the face of any Indian with H1-B visa who came knocking. He had tried everywhere he could think of, and his meager savings were running out. He had to move out of the apartment he was renting in DC after talking to Myles and Anish. They had offered to let him stay with them till he found another job. He had called Anand in California and they had talked at length. Things were as bad for him too; he had taken up a janitorial job at a high school in Oakland, then he was taking acting lessons because he wanted to try his hand out at acting.

"If you want, you could move down here Amit, the change of environment would be good for you, considering your situation with Lisa." Anand had offered a sounding chipper. But Amit had declined graciously thanking him in for the offer. He wanted to make an effort on his own before he could give up and admit defeat. If there was anything he was grateful for, it was the fiercely independent way his father had raised him, nothing was impossible for the man. Absolutely nothing. Amit had learnt in the course of all his losses that the best part of the people you loved would always be with you no matter what happened or where they went. With that Amit had found the strength to go on after his father's funeral. His sister's alliance with the boy she was betrothed to have been moved for a while till all the rites, prayers and offerings had been made for his funeral. This had made Amit a little happy, at least his family was doing well without his father's presence, and he did not feel like such a letdown when he talked to them.

He was walking past a grocery store when he heard someone calling his name. "Is that Amit Khanna I see?!" he stopped and turned around, hoping it was not his mind playing tricks on him out of hunger. The vision he saw made reinforced the soundness of his mind and almost refuted the working of his eyes. It was Manoj, his roommate from freshman year in G-DUB. At least the dark tall guy sprinting towards him with a huge smile looked like him. He had not seen Manoj since he graduated in Amit's sophomore year. They had talked on the phone for a while till life got in the way, the calls got infrequent and then totally petered out. He had changed a lot, the Manoj he remembered was lanky and wore his height and frame with a comfortable easiness, exuding effortless charisma. The man coming towards him as he stood there motionless was a buffed-up God. He had well defined and cut muscles, his hair no longer flopped into his face; he had styled it into a side wave that made him look like Saif Ali Khan from Race. The only thought on Amit's mind as Manoj enveloped him in a bear hug was that this was a man who expected and deserved R-E-S-P-E-C-T.

"It is good to see you Amit!" he smiled widely, his flawless dentition shining through. Amit smiled back overwhelmed by the sight of him. "Manoj it is really you!"

He laughed and punched Amit on the shoulder lightly, "Of course it's me Amit, and did you think I was a ghost?"

Amit laughed loudly and hugged him again. "You are a sight for sore eyes man! Where have you been?"

"I've been back home for about three years," he said shrugging. "The H1-B visa saga was too much to cope with, so I went back home to Delhi and started a clothing line business." Amit looked him over once again with the new information. He looked it; the part of a successful clothes businessman. His navy-blue suit was designer and his shoes spoke quality Italian leather. He looked like he had stepped off the cover of a GQ magazine.

"You look really nice Manoj," he said again tamping down the feeling of failure and disappointment he felt for himself. He hoped the conversation never turned to him, so he would not explain how he had failed to achieve his dreams.

"Let's talk, over tea maybe? We have a lot to catch up on!" everything Manoj said was on an exclamation and his excitement was infectious. It was beginning to rub off on Amit.

"Sure!" he said trying to match Manoj's level of excitement. I know of a place actually, it's not far from here."

"Great, I hope you still don't have an acquired taste for decaf lattes?" he asked with a glint in his eyes. Amit laughed loudly, this was the Manoj he remembered. The happy go lucky fellow he had been had not been lost in all the rigors of responsibility.

The shop was found in Arlington, in a tiny street called Blossom Street. The street had just been reconstructed and new businesses had opened up there. One of them was 'Alix Turner's Cakes and Teas' a quaint little shop Amit had come across on one of his wanderings, he had fallen in love with the quiet peacefulness and homeliness of the café and he was dying to come back and have another taste of Alix's delicious cakes.

"This place is really something Amit, I almost forgot you always had a gift for picking out quality food and restaurants. Did you bring someone special here?" Manoj wiggled his eyebrows at Amit with that ingratiating smile that never left his face.

Amit laughed and waved his comment off, "Oh I wish there was someone special to bring here. I just come here to unwind and eat delicious sweets when I am in the area." Manoj must have picked up on the wistful quality in his voice because he zoned in immediately like a magnifying glass and started probing.

"For you there had always been one-woman Amit, does she still occupy that envied position?"

Amit chuckled, so like Manoj to breach the subjects he did not want to talk about. The man was as he remembered; he had no qualms about prying into your private business and making it his. "You make it sound like I was hopelessly waiting for her to notice me and come rescue me from my pathetic life." He shook his head at his friend and laughed.

"Well that was what it looked like to me after September 11," Manoj was trying very hard to suppress his amusement. "You went about school looking like a four-year-old whose puppy had died."

"I was NOT like that!" Amit screamed, his face showing mock indignation while his lips twitched from barely controlled laughter.

"What can I get you two gentlemen?" Alix asked as she leaned her hip on the back of a seat beside Manoj. This was what Amit liked best about Alix Turner's Café; you got to be served or greeted personally by the owner who was an excellent host. You felt like she knew you and she were invested in your life details. She was a buxom forty- something year old woman with a thick southern accent which she tried really hard to suppress and the effort made people laugh. She always lined her brows with black liner that made her grey eyes seem larger and darker than they really were. Her ears were studded completely with gold rings that gleamed and caught the light whenever she threw her head back to laugh (which was often). Her boisterous laughter was not the only thing that would draw your attention when she was in her element; she also had a dumbbell ring in the inner parts of her lower lip which was golden too. Her arms were also covered in tribal tattoos which she would talk about to everyone who would just care to listen.

Right now, she was staring at Manoj as if he were her next meal which was funny for Amit to watch, these smoldering eyes she was trying to affect as she tried to flirt with him came off looking ghoulish and ridiculous.

"Hmmm, it has been so long since I had me some really good-looking men in here. What is your name sonny?" her attention was beginning to fluster Manoj who looked at Amit for some help. Amit shook his head at him discreetly as if to say, 'you are in this alone buddy'.

"Hmm, Manoj ma'am" he smiled uneasily, keeping his arms in his lap like a good boy afraid she would grab it too. Amit was red in the face from trying to suppress his mirth at his friend's predicament. Alix ran her hands the length of his shoulder and cooed delightedly, "A fine name for a fine man. Tell me; do you have a lady to go home to sonny? It would be a shame to let all this…fineness to go to waste."

Amit could not hold it in anymore; he burst into a fit of convulsive laughter, hitting his thighs with his palms as he laughed at Manoj's expense. As if on cue, Alix dropped the act immediately and joined in the laughter. Manoj looked from one laughing face to another; only just comprehending the fact that he had just been played.

"Got you good and nice didn't I sonny?" she said after she had recovered slightly from her laughing jag. "Easy honey, I was not going to eat you." Her surprisingly white teeth shone bright with the mirth she felt. She turned and high fived Amit who was still doubled over in laughter. When he had controlled himself sort of, he coughed and apologized.

"I'm sorry Manoj, she does that to all her new customers, especially the good-looking ones. I guess you could take this as some sort of backhanded compliment. She really likes you." He continued to chuckle as he talked. Manoj shook his head, the frown on his face refusing to stay on. He tried and failed to appear angry because Alix really was a clown and she stayed by their table chit chatting for a while before she took their orders.

"Would you want the house's special today? It's a shepherd pie, and I would vouch for it with my integrity." She said after putting down their drink orders. Amit had asked for a decaf latte as expected and Manoj had stuck to mint green tea. "We would take your word for it Alix" Amit said, and she left swaying her hips with exaggerated movements. She turned suddenly and caught them staring at her and she winked at them before disappearing.

"Is she always this...hyper?" Manoj asked with a slight shudder and Amit laughed nodding. "On some days her husband joins in the fun, creating a ruckus in here. Manoj shuddered again, trying to imagine two of Alix in this quaint little place. He wondered how they kept it so peaceful when its owner was such a handful. She returned with their steaming hot drinks within a few minutes as if she had conjured it up and left to attend to another customer who just walked in. Manoj watched in awe as she turned on her charm once again and swept this new customer off his feet with her wit. No wonder they all came back for more. He could see Amit was hooked and he told him as much.

"It's not just the character and larger than life presence of the owner Manoj, the café also has some 'character' too. And they do serve really good pastries." Manoj nodded taking a sip of his tea.

"So, Amit, you never really did answer my question." He looked at him intently.

"What question?" Amit stalled, dreading the question he had to answer. It was typical of Manoj to not let go of an issue till he had addressed it to his satisfaction. Amit should have learned his lesson; delay and avoidance tactics had never worked on Manoj, not then and certainly not now.

"It is hard to forget the question I asked about Lisa seeing as you still drink her coffee and everything."

Amit laughed and shook his head, "You are like a dog with a bone Manoj." Manoj did not reply, his gaze on Amit's face with his brows raised to meet his hairline.

With a sigh of defeat Amit shrugged, "I guess she is fine, I used to work with her." At that Manoj raised his brows intrigued. "Oh wow, I did not see that coming." Amit went on to tell him how he had run into her after an interview at MetroTech and how things have gone on between them since leaving out the fact that she was living with another guy all the while.

"It must have been something to be rejected twice by the same woman, huh?" Amit shrugged as if it did not matter anymore. "I always thought you guys would snap out of your silliness and end up getting married. I had no idea you would still be pining four years down the road." Amit lifted a shoulder while he sipped on his latte and said nothing else. Their intermittent silence was filled thankfully by the arrival of their shepherd pie which looked like a casserole to Manoj. He reluctantly took a bite and he moaned, Amit was right about Alix Turner's pastries. Amit who seemed to be waiting for his opinion of the pie grinned with an 'I told you so' look.

"This is heavenly, Amit." He said amidst the mouthful he was trying to hold down while he spooned up another bite. "You really don't play with your food, do you?"

"I smell good food from a hundred miles away." He shrugged. "So Manoj, what are you doing back in the States?"

"A fashion show, some of the brands I stock are holding a fashion show this Saturday and I had to come for business promotion."

"Does that mean business is going well yeah?"

"We try our best." He laughed trying to be modest.

"So Manoj, do you have someone in your life now? Back home maybe?"

Manoj just laughed shaking off the question, "No one yet man, too busy." Their conversation went on to several other things as they played catch up. They discussed the current H1b visa laws in America and how it had affected Amit and a lot of other Indians they knew. He went on to give him updates on some of their friends from college and their whereabouts now. Before he left, Manoj weaseled out a promise from Amit to stay in touch again and they parted ways. Amit didn't feel so bad about his predicament after it all. He guessed he had just been a victim of circumstances and he was not going to feel less than adequate because he was in between jobs while some of his friends were living the life.

CHAPTER 11- BREAKING EVEN

It had been six months since Amit was laid off of work, and all he could hear is rejection from American companies. Although he had done some coding in school he did not have the required work experience as a programmer. Also, he had concerns that if he will go back to India as an unsuccessful person, people would make his life a living hell. The good thing about America was that no job was considered small or of lower respect. Even the janitor at the University owned a car and was respected by students and teachers. In India that was not the case as the lower class did not have the money to buy a car or scooter in some cases. Most of the companies did not even give him an opportunity to interview since he required H1-B visa. Slowly his options to survive were running out. For most of the illegal Indians the option was to work at a grocery store, gas station, Indian restaurants or Motels. He started searching for Indian businesses on the internet. "Hi! My name is Amit and I am looking for a job" That became Amit's punch line. After making 100+ phone calls, he received a call back from a Sri Lankan businessman whose name was Prabhakar and was looking for someone to manage finances for his run-down strip bar. This was not easy for him to take this job since this would have required him to lie in front of his mother. Since Amit was desperate and was on the verge of homelessness he took this job thinking that one day he will be able to find a better job. He was told by Prabhakar that he will be just responsible for managing finances and has a separate wait and restaurant staff.

Amit was relieved that he finally had a job although he had some anxiety of what he was getting into. The shift time was from 4 PM to midnight which was odd considering he was just a finance guy and not a cashier/bartender. Any ways he reached the bar at 3:45 PM where he was welcomed by a scantily clad lady named Sunny. Sunny was a 35-year-old lady from Delhi who helped Prabhakar in selecting the strippers, managing the wardrobe and make-up for them. Strippers worked as contractors and had to pay the club owner for dancing at the bar. There was a selection process which was headed by Prabhakar and Sunny. In order to be competitive, the scouts were sent all over the World to get beautiful girls from Russia, Europe and Latin American countries. The work visa was arranged for some and some entered through Mexican border. 80% of the strip bars were run by Mafia, Politicians or Hotel Business Tycoons (Mr. Trump had stakes in a lot of strip bars).

Sunny with her fake American accent asked, "Are you the new cashier?" Amit looked confused but responded "I am the Finance Manager" Sunny chuckled and responded, "Same thing, Buddy" Sunny took him inside and he was amazed by the lights and thumping music. The bar was colorful and so were the bikini clad women complementing the lights. Although Amit was tempted to look at them he was more interested in proving his work ethic to Prabhakar.

First day/night at the job was exciting as he was surrounded by scantily clad women and all he had to do is collect cash at the counter while making an entry at the register. There were 2 Bouncers whose names were Omar and Moby (both were from one of the African countries) who stood at the gate to check ID cards etc. Both of them were muscular and had the stare to scare anyone away. Their job was also to make sure that drunk patrons were kicked out of the bar. At the end of the night a shiny Mercedes stopped in front of the bar and Prabhakar stepped out of the car. He was dressed in a white suit and a hat to complement his suit. He was a shrewd businessman ready to go to any extent for money. He used to come every other night to check the cash in the register and make sure that his staff was not cheating him.

Amit started enjoying his work (although it was demanding, and the hours were odd) he learned the art of customer service, dealing with difficult people and also was exposed to the Underworld scene of United States.

"Do you carry coke? "Asked a patron. Amit responded, "They have everything at the bar." To which Joe responded, "Not that kind of coke." Amit did not know this side of the business as Prabhakar had kept this as a secret for select few. His overseas trips not only included scouting for strippers, but also for coke and other drugs. Inside the VIP room (rate was up to 5000$ for an hour) the patrons got their stripper and drugs fix and this was done in such a clandestine manner that a lot of employees did not know. Anyways Joe entered the bar and was greeted by the Bartender. He was a regular and therefore the Bartender and Strippers loved him. He had a knack for carrying interesting conversation with the stripper community and often had VIP dances with his favorites.

There was also a separate room where a lot of beautiful strippers from Russia and South American countries did more than lap dances. These women were from poor families in their home countries and this was an easier way to earn quick money. There were special entry cards for this room and the entry list was maintained by Prabhakar. Amit had no clue what he was getting into when he had accepted the job.

"Can I get a special dance?" asked a customer. Lisa who was an experienced stripper responded "Sure, 500$ for VIP room ½ hour and 1000$ for an hour." Customer responded, "How about if I want an E topping on that?" Lisa had vague idea that drugs were being offered in the VIP room, but she was not comfortable with these topics as there was always a fear of cops (E was the street name for Ecstasy which was a popular drug at that time). Lisa quickly ran to Sean (One of the bartenders) who was one of Prabby's (that was Prabhakar's nick name) confidant. Lisa took the customer to the VIP room and E pills were ready on the table for the customer. "Hands up" screamed the customer. Lisa was shocked as no customer had acted like that in the past. What Lisa did not know that the customer was a local cop who was working off of a tip received from an informer. "Cops!" Lisa screamed at the top of her lungs which got the attention of the bouncers standing outside the VIP room.

The cops stormed through the front door and immediately people started running outside. Amit and a lot of other staff were arrested and taken in the cop cars along with Prabhakar. The interrogation session started at 1 AM which lasted till 7 AM. All the others were let go except Prabhakar and Sunny as they had stakes in business.

Amit was back on the street although he was grateful that the cops did not ask him about his visa status or any other details. Most of them did not have any criminal records and were just listed as employees. He thanked God that he did not get into trouble and went to the closest temple to pray Lord Krishna.

Joe, one of the bar helpers had developed friendship with Amit and was able to get Amit into a restaurant as a wait staff. He was happy that he was able to find a job so quickly after that debacle. The Sweet Haven which was one of a chain of restaurants owned by an old war veteran named Jason Conrad who had fought in the Vietnam War. The restaurant was now managed by his son Jason Conrad Jr. The pay was not so great, but it was enough to pay the rent and get some necessary things as his savings were dwindling. He had sent home his severance pay to help pay for his sister's dowry, so he needed a job of any kind then. He had also moved into a studio apartment in DC that was in a quiet and relatively safe environment. Relatively safe in the sense that the people who lived there were on the down low and everyone tried to mind their business.

The Sweet Haven restaurant was beautiful; Amit had always believed that one of the greatest inducers of a healthy appetite was a good environment and he did not just mean a simply decent environment, he extolled the place of aesthetics in restaurant business. The place had high ceilings with stained glass, and it was decorated somewhat like the smaller less elaborate model of the Sistine chapel in Italy with some of its grandeur and elegance. The chairs were ruby red velvet cushions in a gold high seat and a small round table that could accommodate four chairs each. They had a bar lining the far wall of the eating space and the flowers that adorned the tables were fresh and replaced after every shift, so it remained very fresh and crisp like perpetual spring. Even the name seemed appropriate, one had the sense of being in a safe place which would cater to one's comfort needs and help one have a sweet memory.

Amit believed one of the reasons Jason Conrad Jr. hired him was how he had praised the restaurant décor and style of designing with so much awe and excitement. He had probably also been impressed with how much he knew about restaurant business, especially Asian and French cuisine. "You have potential for a successful restaurant business if you want Amit Khanna." he had said as he shook his hand. Amit loved waiting tables here; they had to wear fancy tuxedos and tail coats every day at work. It gave him the opportunity to dress up since he hardly had anywhere to go after work. The only other place Amit ever went was the second job he had on the side with a cab driving company. He had gotten this job from a friend of Anish's who had put out word that his uncle needed new drivers for his cab driving service. Amit had been grateful for the opportunity to earn some extra income to augment his savings.

He drove the cab in the early evenings before going for his night shifts at the Sweet Haven. He loved the unique experiences he got from the numerous customers he had met. He had always been a people watcher and he never lost an opportunity to find out what made people tick. He found it amusing when people reacted in a strange way to him because of his race and color. He had heard a lot of things people said ranging from; "wow, I bet in India you guys abhor battles and all that because of…. You know, Gandhi. The non-violence campaign and all that stuff." "Oh, like how many gods do you guys worship back home? There has to be about a hundred of them, right?" that question had been priceless, and instead of getting offended, Amit had found it extremely amusing. The customer had been a drunken woman who probably was in academia. She was apparently the chatty type when she was inebriated.

"Actually, we worship about a hundred thousand of them in my culture and we have holidays for all of them." Amit had said with a straight face. "Every single one of them?!" she had exclaimed, her unfocused eyes getting really big with fascination.

"Yes ma'am, every one of them."

"Hmmm, that must be nice." She sighed expressively and rolled her head to the side lazily. He felt sorry for her and the hangover she would battle with in the morning. When he had gotten to her address, he had to carry her into the house since she could not stand on her own. He had to open her purse by her drunken directives to get his pay. He could not help thinking some Americans were careless and too trusting. He could have been a serial killer or a thief and could have killed her or stolen from her and she would not remember a thing. He even doubted she would remember the cab service she had hired that night, but he had been taught integrity, it was ingrained in him and stealing from an unconscious woman was a bad as kicking a sick cow.

There had been this one customer who had challenged him to think outside the box of the existence he had carved out for himself. It was a silver haired man who was probably in his sixties. He lived in Chicago, but he came to Washington DC often for conferences and meetings. Instead of using a rental car service, he preferred a cab service and he always requested for Amit to drive him around when he was in town. He always gave him huge tips for the company and conversation he enjoyed in Amit's service and Amit liked the man too. He was the only person who had taken a genuine interest in Amit which was not an idle curiosity to ask him if he worshipped cows too or if he knew some certain random friend they had met on some social media site and figured India was so small Amit must have met them too.

Mr. Liam Carell would call him when he got on his flight and then he would wait at the airport till he got off the plane and he would take him to his usual reserved room at the Fairmont Olympic Hotel. He would collect his itinerary and work round the man's schedule while swapping duty at the Sweet Haven. Amit had even scored Mr. Carell as a customer at Sweet Haven. Their trips were always interesting with captivating discussions. "What is your take on the current World trade exchange rates and America's stake in it Amit?" he would ask as a typical conversation opener and then the floor was open. Amit enjoyed conversing with him, Mr. Carell reminded him of his Algorithms professor Mr. Patel. On some occasions, he had invited Amit up to his room to have coffee with him as they discussed some more but Amit had always declined the invitation.

"Sir it would be more convenient for our working relationship if there is no abuse of it by over familiarization. I would much prefer the boundaries remain clear cut." He had said to Mr. Carell politely. The man had laughed and nodded his acquiescence, "You have good work ethics Amit, I like that. You would go very far if you met the right people."

"I believe you are part of the right crowd sir." Amit had said with a courteous laugh.

"You are witty too! I like that." Mr. Carell had replied on a chuckle as he waved him away.

On one of their trips, Mr. Carell had asked him a question, "You know so much about the restaurant business as I have seen Amit, why are you not running one?" the question had fallen out of the companionable silence they had been enjoying and Amit wondered what might have brought it on. The man was also staring at him intently through the rear-view mirror waiting for his answer.

"Sir, I just have not given it so much of a thought. I would love to own one someday, but I don't have much capital saved up for the business if I wanted to venture in. I guess I am trying to save up."

"How?"

"Uhmmm, excuse me sir?"

"You said you were saving up for the business Amit, I want to know what your saving plans are and how long it would take you to 'save up'" the man said the last two words with affected mockery.

Amit got flustered, "Well if you put it that way sir, I guess I don't have much of a plan of action."

"Because it looks to me that you are just trying to get by. Are you going to drive cabs and wait tables all your life?"

"I really did not think about it like that sir." He said hoping he had not destroyed the notion Mr. Carell had of him. Just like that, the conversation had been abruptly terminated and they returned to the ambient silence they had been enjoying. Now, Amit was not relaxed, his mental wheels were whirring at break neck speed as he tried to analyze his spending and savings. Mr. Carell was right, at the rate he was going he would not have anything saved up for another 10 years still. He knew this was the man's motive for raising up the topic; to get him to think and formulate a good plan. The man was a master at passive aggressive leadership and decision making. When he dropped him off at the Fairmont Hotel, he tapped him on the shoulder as he got down. "I know you would formulate a failsafe business plan Amit, you are so much better than this." With that he went into the hotel reception without another glance back.

The next day after doing his research all night, Amit approached his boss Mr. Jason Conrad Sr. and asked for some advice. The man was a pleasant old man in his eighties and he stayed around in the Washington DC branch of the restaurant chain because this was where his home was. He helped with the kitchen staff and entertained some of the guests. Everyone loved him for his simplicity and friendliness and that was probably what gave Amit the boldness for approach. The man looked him over for a while thoughtfully through his rheumy eyes, "You really are serious aren't you Amit?"

"Yes sir, I just want some pointers on how to start up a big restaurant business. I would be grateful for anything you could tell me." His tone was earnest and fearful; he was afraid the elderly man would be offended by his request or would consider him a threat to his business.

The old man nodded and smiled at him. He gripped Amit's hands with his slightly shaking ones and peered at his face. "I will tell you something I know for sure sonny, the World and all its variables are unsteady and unreliable, but what you have inside of you, the goodness inside your heart is what you can take to the bank. And you, you are a force son. You have the drive to succeed and your heart is in the right place, don't lose it."

Amit was overwhelmed by his kind words and his acceptance meant a lot to Amit. He had received so much love from some of the people here that it had compensated for the cruelty and misfortune he had suffered too.

Much to Amit's pleasure and surprise, he gave him what he wanted; answered all his questions and told him how he had started a small restaurant with a disabling injury from war, post-traumatic stress disorder, and a very big dream. Amit was overwhelmed by all the man had shared with him and he was grateful to sit and visit with him for a while longer before his shift started. He found out the old man still came into the restaurant because he did not want to battle with loneliness and he didn't want to be fully dependent on his son.

"I'm retired not dead boy, I don't need to have Jared breathing down my neck and hovering over me like an invalid." He said in answer to Amit's direct question on why he did not just live with his son instead of taking the trouble to come in every morning. The way he said the word 'invalid' so abhorrently made Amit laugh so hard at his spunk. This old man's story inspired Amit to pursue his dreams and not remain content with mediocrity and settling for a life he felt he could have instead of the one he could have.

The next day, he took his business plan with him when he was asked to pick up Liam Carell at the Fairmont Olympic Hotel. He was very excited to show the man what he had come up with; he had never felt this fired up about anything in his life. He would note down some of the few things he had learned from this experience; his dream had never looked more achievable and powerful than now it was written down. He could not agree more with a motivational speaker he had once listened to; Steve Chandler who had said 'dreams gain power when you write it down, more power every time you write it down.' He had just never put that theory to practice till now.

When he showed Mr. Carell the plans, the man studied the paper for a while in the cab's overhead light and passed it back to him wordlessly while he went on punching stuff on his laptop. After a while he must have seen Amit's questioning glance in the rear-view mirror and then he shrugged at him and said, "Not bad." With a shrug.

Amit was confused; he could not understand why the man was being suddenly morose and quiet. He was the one who had challenged Amit to put down a business plan and his capital funding strategies. He had even gone to the trouble of talking to his boss' father about restaurant business and all he was getting from the man was a 'not bad'?!

"Is that all you have to say sir?" Amit asked not a little disgruntled. He looked up again, his eyes direct and piercing even in the rear-view mirror. "It's not a bad plan yes Amit, but I could punch big holes in it. You have a lot to learn, but these lessons are better experienced than taught."

The rest of their journey was completed in silence as Amit stewed in his juices, completely confused about what was going on with his elderly friend. He went on through to tell him about his plan to apply for loans and look for investors. He would not let the man discourage him after he had given him the push to start in the first place.

Liam Carell looked up before he got off when he got to his destination; "Amit, can you come in for a second; I have a little time before my first meeting."

"Ok Sir," he said wondering what this was about. Had he annoyed the man in the course of the drive or was his attempt at a business plan so abhorrent the man was unimpressed by him? He hoped that whatever it was, it was not any of the options he had just considered. Mr. Carell led him to an empty board room at the Washington DC Justice Centre and gave him a seat. Amit had never been in the Justice Centre before and he had wondered what the inside of the building looked like. The halls they passed through were white with a clinical harshness that could hurt the eyes and people milled around busily not noticing the people they passed. It was like a beehive in here with the way everyone was dressed in similar clothes and seemed to be in a hurry. The only people who paid attention to the comings in and goings out was the security detail. They had blocked Amit as he had stepped in, the prejudice shining in their eyes, "its ok guys, he's with me." Mr. Carell had said with a lazy smile, tapping one of the men on the chest.

"One would think with all the talk about the eradication of racism that the discrimination would really stop." He muttered under his breath as he led Amit through a white hall to the empty board room. He sat down at the head of the long mahogany table and motioned wordlessly for Amit to sit. He brought out some papers and passed it on to Amit with an enigmatic expression. Amit looked through the papers not fully comprehending what he saw there. He looked up at the man with a quizzical look in his eyes.

"I actually liked your business plan Amit and I would want to be your first investor." He motioned to the papers he had passed on to Amit, "That is a written agreement with the percentage of profit I would be getting at the end of the year along with a progress report. I believe you would make it in this business."

Amit stared at him as if he had grown two or maybe even three heads. He could not believe his luck! He looked through the documents again with new eyes, thinking he was probably hallucinating. But everything was there as he said. He had been blessed with kindness really in this country where he had almost lost his dream. "Rea ...Really sir?" he asked, maybe seeking an explanation or maybe a catch in this offer that was too good to be true.

Mr. Carell nodded with a smile. "I did say you had a lot to learn......from experience." Amit released something that sounded like a moan or a cry; - he really could not figure out what sound his throat was producing nor did he care- and went down on his knees clasping his hands in front of his face. "Thank you so much sir!" he touched Mr. Carell's feet and the man withdrew it laughing.

"I do know a little about Indian religion and culture Amit, and I would much prefer not to be worshipped." The man chuckled as he stood up, pulling Amit up with him. He looked him in the eyes when he had pulled him fully to his feet and held up his shoulders. "Go be more Amit, you are much better than this life," He gestured to Amit's face generally. He gave him a pat on the back as he left. Amit stood there for a while with the check that had been among the documents he had been given. He had issued him a check of two million dollars to start up. Amit knew the amount could not be sufficient to fund the whole business, but it was a good place to start. He was overcome with emotion, but he tried to pull himself together. God had really blessed him with wonderful people and little favors that looked small but were really big.

He walked out of the office with a spring in his step armed with an idea on how to start. He went straight to his boss at the cab services and put in his notice. Then he took a ride to work at Sweet haven for his evening shift. All the while, he was busily strategizing in his head and putting things in place on how to go about getting a place. He always had a notepad for taking orders while waiting tables at Sweet Haven, but for him it had only been a formality; he rarely wrote orders down there because he never forgot orders or got them mixed up. But this night he was writing things down furiously and he was slightly unfocused and absent minded.

"Are you OK Amit?" Justin the sous chef who took the orders from Amit asked. They had struck up a friendship of sorts because he was the only one Amit talked to regularly. The sweet haven was not like Joe Sacchin's where everyone knew everyone else and they made friends easily because it was a school environment and most of them had a lot in common. Here, everyone was courteous to each other and they tried their best to work synchronously, but they hardly pursued a friendship outside of work. But with Justin and Amit, they had had to talk more often because of the relationship between their jobs and tidbits of information about themselves had trickled into some of their conversation and they could be considered friends somewhat.

"You look out of sorts to me today, what's going on?" he frowned as he studied Amit. "Even your eyes seem…. wild." he could not help but notice too as Amit handed in the order he was given by a young family out by the private booth.

Amit laughed heartily at his concern, "Really? I look unfocused to you?" his grin got wider as he asked.

"Your face is glowing man, what's up?"

"What if I told you to come work for me Justin and offered to pay you 20% more than you are being paid here, would you come?" he asked his eyes shining. Justin studied him skeptically, as if gauging his mental health.

"Have you been drinking Amit? You could be fired for that alone." The question made Amit laugh even more.

"You really think I'm drunk?" he looked at Justin with an accommodating smile. "You remember telling me your biggest dream was to be your own chef in a big restaurant and to make your own recipe book?" Justin nodded, wondering what that had to do with anything.

"What if I tell you that I could make your dreams come true?" He whispered fiercely to the other man, so he would not be overheard.

"How would you be able to do that?" he asked still skeptical. Amit leveled a glance at him in exasperation. "Have you not been listening to the things I have said?"

He went on to share part of his plan with Justin and offered to give him a job as his head chef at the restaurant. Justin was still not fully convinced Amit was not playing around, but he was sold on the offer and he wanted to be his own boss in his own kitchen. So, Amit scored his first employee within the first day of getting his plan underway. Next on his agenda was to call a Realtor to help him find a building to buy and then some more investors.

****
****

Within the next two weeks, Amit went to see twelve buildings he could probably buy/lease for the business. But only about five of them could fit what he was looking to build. The first one was an old repossessed warehouse, but it was in an industrial neighborhood. The second one used to be a conference hall, but it was not as big as Amit hoped on the inside plus the maintenance bills would take up almost all the money he had, and investors were not really pouring in. The other three buildings were all warehouses with a lot of maintenance and renovation bills, but they could be cut to fit into the mold he wanted.

"There are more places we could look at in Fairfax and maybe Ashburn if you would be willing to look that far sir." The Realtor offered when they had gone to see the last warehouse in the Alexandria area that day before his shift at Sweet Haven. But he declined; "Maybe tomorrow, Ms. Steven." Amit thanked her and left the building a little disgruntled. He had been expecting to feel something when he saw the right place. He did not know what to call this; instinct or maybe even a gut feeling, but he hoped something would click when his restaurant came but as of now, nothing had happened yet. He pushed this out of his mind as he made a mental note to talk to his lawyer when he got off work. The building he wanted would show up when it wanted. His major worry was to get investors. He had pitched to some company directors but still none of them had gotten back to him. He hoped that would not be the case for very long.

He was trying to cross the road when someone tapped him, "would you care to read the paper sir?" it was a young boy, he could pass for fifteen but only barely. He looked gaunt and unkempt, but Amit could see the pride in the set of his shoulders and the clench of his jaw. This was a boy who would not take handouts from the World. Something in Amit softened when he looked at the boy and he took the paper he had offered him without a word. "Its three dollars sir," he said still looking at Amit with an enigmatic expression. Amit dipped his hand in his pocket and pulled out a ten-dollar bill and pressed it into his hand. Amit squeezed the boy's hands with both of his when he saw the reluctance in his eyes to collect the money. "Please take it." He said and left with his newspaper clutched in his armpit.

He got into a bus and took the seat at the back; he was not in a hurry to get to work because his shift would not begin till around two hours from then. He opened his paper to give the impression of busyness, so he would not be disturbed by anyone who wanted to chat. He needed to be alone with his thoughts. Halfway through the paper, he came across an ad about an old mansion that was up for sale at a giveaway price. Amit's heart started beating fast as he read the ad, it stated that the house was about eight thousand square feet plus it had a driveway which could be turned into a parking lot. The picture on the Ad showed a rundown house with its front porch falling in but it was in a safe place that could be approved by the Washington DC Health and Sanitation department. He checked his time, he still had about one hour before his shift started at Sweet Haven, so he got down at the next stop and took a cab to the address to the mansion. It was just as the pictures showed, he tried to control the thrill of excitement coursing through him; he had finally found his perfect restaurant space! Things were finally falling into place.

CHAPTER 12- ROCK BOTTOM

When the building was bought, and the renovation had gotten underway, a miracle came in the form of a sole investor who was ready to invest in the business for 45% shares of the company which was fair considering what he was bringing to the table. Amit asked his lawyer Alicia Temple to look through the contract the man had brought to be signed. The man, Jayesh Patel was in the grocery store business and he was looking to expand his business to include food, he had told Amit so. He was a lanky man with a thick Gujrati accent (he had married the daughter of a rich motel owner and that's how inherited a lot of money from his father-in-law). Gujrati community was pretty big in United States and they owned 75% of the motels and Indian grocery stores in United States.

In America, Patels were that ethnic group who became entrenched in a clearly identifiable economic sector, working at jobs for which it had no evident cultural, geographical or even racial affinity. Italians owning pizzerias, or Japanese people running judo schools was a no-brainer but there were some other obvious examples of this. There was Korean dominance of the deli-and-grocery sector in New York -- a city where the Chinese run most laundries and Sri Lankans, ran most porn-video stores. Or the Arabs in greater Detroit, who have a stranglehold on gas stations, or the Vietnamese who monopolize nail salons in Los Angeles, the security guards outside New Delhi's more affluent residences, virtually all of whom are Nepalese; or the prostitutes in the United Arab Emirates, who are so often women from Russia.

According to the figures from the Asian American Hotel Owners Association (A.A.H.O.A.), slightly more than 50 percent of all motels in the United States were owned by people of Indian origin. Indians constituted less than 1 percent of America's population, the conquest of this economic niche appeared extraordinary.

"I saw the pitch you gave KFC and I was impressed, this city lacks good Indian restaurants with quality traditional Indian dishes because the food is prepared by South Americans who know very little about Indian cuisine and served tasteless food. It would be nice to have traditional Indian dishes in this side of the country. People would jump at the novelty of it, and that is what I want to invest in." the man had said when he came to meet Amit and just like that; Khanna's Dish n' Spice was underway.

Amit also hired a friend of Anand's who was a great chef in California, but he needed to move down to Washington DC to be closer to his parents. His name was Devdas and the man was in his thirties. Amit contracted him to train Justin in more exotic and spicy Indian food and offered him the position of the sous chef with a pay of 10$ an hour which was pretty fair considering that this was a new business. He hired an assistant to help him with the client and staff relationship while he controlled the administrative and accounting part of the restaurant as well as making sure the quality of their food never went down.

Within one year, Amit's labor paid off, people did find Indian food intriguing and were eager to test it. The Indian community in Washington DC soon started flocking into the restaurant in droves, hungry for that lost taste of home they had left behind. The public's favorite seemed to be his special recipe for Tandoori Chicken which was taught by his grand mom. All in all, business was booming and all the hours he put into the recipes paid off. Amit was over the moon, he had the life he had always wanted even though it had not quite come in the package he had expected but he deserved the new turn his life had taken. Now he had direction, purpose, focus. He was confident nothing could bring it down, but how wrong he was.

****
****

Because Amit's H1-b Visa had expired, and he could not apply for a permanent residency permit (green card), he and Jayesh Patel had agreed with the consent of Mr. Liam Carell to register the business under Mr. Patel's name. At the time the decision had been made, it had seemed like the most reasonable decision to make. Amit had hoped that by the time his H1- B visa expired, he would be able to apply for the green card as an EB-1 or an EB-3 perhaps with Carell's help. His plans had seemed fail safe until the shit hit the fan and things went downhill from there.

When Khanna's Dish 'n' Spice had opened in downtown DC, the local restaurant businesses there had not predicted its success at all. Their forecast had been doom and gloom, but Amit had ignored them, building from the scratch anything that needed to be built. Amit led by example; spending more than 80% of his time in the restaurant than he ever slept or socialized. His hard work had paid off, much to the disappointment and chagrin of the local food businesses around. Amit could not understand why they were so disgruntled, his clientele was quite different. He catered to the people who came because they loved Indian cuisine. The problem may have arisen from the fact that most everyone in the area had come into the restaurant, some out of curiosity and some out of their acquired taste for Indian food and sweets.

These people did not hide their displeasure and hatred from Amit, some would scratch Amit's car in the parking lot and some went as far as coming into the restaurant to rain abuses on the staff and customers. Part of their hang-ups was the fact that the owner of this very successful business venture was a man of color and so according to them; 'he did not have a right to live in this country let alone taking over their local businesses'. One of those men had made quite an impression on Amit and the workers. He had come into the restaurant looking like a homeless beggar with the stench of stale booze and something else on his clothes and in his breath. He had taken a seat at a table for two and had refused to order anything. After a while, when nobody paid him so much attention, he began making quite a ruckus, complaining about why the whole place smelled so much.

"Ughh, it stinks in here! Maybe it's a technical problem somewhere, can't you fix it?" he had jeered at one of Amit's waiters who was still so courteous and was trying to quiet him down. When the other guests had looked at him distastefully or told him to shut up, he had a comeback; "Are you guys sure you do not have poop in your food?" he smirked at them.

"I'm going to ask you to leave now sir." But he sneered at the man and refused to leave. When they wanted to escort him out, he had started to kick around breaking stuff with his hands and feet. He kicked so hard at one of the glass windows it shattered and cut one of the customers. The police were called immediately, and he was taken out.

Amit refused to press charges and the man got out on bail. Two days later, the DC Food Inspection came to inspect the restaurant and its environs. There were two of them; an African American woman and a blonde who had the stance of a cop. They searched everything, from the kitchen, to the waste disposal and then to the vents. When they were done, they asked to interview Amit privately.

He took them to his office out back, amidst the questioning glances of his employees. "Mr. Amit Khanna am I right?" the blonde muscled guy said while looking around at his office. The place was small but cozy, Amit tried to see it through their foreign eyes. It sure would look uncomfortable and stuffy to them, so he did not blame them for their distasteful glances.

"Yes sir, I hope there is no problem" the man just shrugged as the lady passed Amit an identification form with his name on it. It says here that your student visa expired about three years ago sir." She said looking at him sternly. "Do you know anything about this Mr. Khanna?"

Amit frowned and collected the folder from him, she was right; there was no record of his H1-B visa anywhere on the form. "But I have a work visa permit here that was issued 4 years ago." He produced his H1- B visa stamped on the passport to them. She collected it and examined it silently before making a call to run the identification numbers on the card and it was confirmed that the numbers were never registered.

Blood left Amit's head as he looked at them, this could not be happening to him. "I'm sure there is a mistake somewhere sir, I was issued that visa by a consulting company.

"Which one?" the guy spoke up now.

"E.B. Consulting Company here in Virginia."

At the mention of the company they exchanged a tight glance and she turned back to him with a grave expression on her face. "E.B. Consulting was shut down about a year ago and their facilities repossessed by the US government because of their illegal dealings and forgery. Satish Sharma is in federal prison right now. She watched him intently for a reaction to that news, as she delivered it. "I'm afraid we would have to take you into police custody sir." She said then.

Amit nodded and went with them after calling Jayesh Patel and leaving a message for Mr. Liam Carell. He asked the employers to get back to work and he put Justin in charge as he left.

The holding cell he was kept in was cold and moldy, with a concrete slab for a seat and a desk that was built into the floor. The place could only boast of one large glass window that looked like it could somehow serve as an interrogation front. And from that large glass window, he could see into some offices and he watched them idly bustling around. Occasionally, someone came in to lay a complaint and was led into an office. Three other people were arrested as he waited in that cell. To pass time; he counted every dot and mole on the ceiling, memorizing every crack on it. He played the number game, counting to a thousand and starting all over again. He soon got tired of that game when he had counted his hundredth thousand. He refused to be conscious of the time he was being kept and he refused to consider the worst outcome in this situation. It had been a long time he practiced some meditation, so he took the opportunity to meditate.

When they finally opened his cell door, he was vaguely conscious that he had spent about 8 hours in there and his whole lower body was stiff with inactivity even though he had tried not to check the time, he still had kept count. He hoped he was able to stand up when the time came.

The two officers from the food hygiene agency came into the holding cell along with two male police officers and his lawyer Alicia while Jayesh Patel brought up the rear. After they were all seated, the elderly police officer introduced himself as agent Burton and his colleague as Agent Smith.

"It's bad, Mr. Khanna" he said going straight to the point. Your stay in the United States have been illegal for three years now sir, and even if your visa was authentic, it was a work visa and you could not operate a business with it."

Amit wanted to answer and defend himself when Alicia kicked his leg under the table, "I will take it from here sir." He watched her try to find an angle for him or a loophole that could help them avoid the inevitable fate that met anyone in this situation; deportation.

They had talked for a long while and nothing was yielding even with Jayesh Patel's supposed influence. Amit asked if they could speak to Liam Carell and Alicia gave him a sad look, "Mr. Carell is fighting for his life in the hospital, Amit. He had a heart failure."

Amit looked at her flummoxed; everything could not go down the drain just like that. His life here could not have gone downhill so fast! This could not be happening to him. He asked for some privacy to speak to his business partner Jayesh and he was granted it. When everybody had left, he came close to Jayesh and grabbed his hand.

"Please, you have to help me get out of here! Surely you can do something." He pleaded. Jayesh shook his head and withdrew his hand, giving him a baleful stare.

"One would think you would be more careful, why did you never check out the visa you had been given? How could you drag me into this mess?" Amit stared at him, not believing what he was hearing. He was blaming him?! Amit tried to remain calm and ask for help again. "Is it not too late to cast blames? Please can you do something, anything! I can't lose everything"

"I'm sorry, I can't help you Khanna, and I can do one thing though." Hope surged through Amit as he stared at the man, expecting a lifeline of any kind. "I would be willing to buy you out, for a fair price." He said with a straight face.

Amit fell back in his chair like he had just been sucker punched, he stared at Mr. Patel open mouthed not believing the cruelty in that one statement. How could he not have seen this coming, not seen this side of the man he had led into his business!

"It's a fair offer considering you would be deported after all and the business would still be mine, I am giving you an opportunity to get some of the money you invested back."

"You can't make that decision alone, you need Mr. Carell's signature too."

"Oh that," he said his smile sinister. "Mr. Carell has agreed to sell his shares to me too, I met him a few days ago and he has signed the document with the assumption that it was your idea." He smiled at Amit.

It took Amit a while, staring at the man before it dawned on him. This was all him! The answering smile on Patel's face at the shocking realization in Amit's own confirmed it. Everything became clear to Amit now. The slimy bastard had tricked a sick man into signing an agreement to sell his shares – he did not want to imagine the sick manipulative ways he had used to get that done- and he had now reported the restaurant and Amit to the authorities because he probably had done a background check on Amit.

Amit wanted to scream and curse and cry, but he controlled his trembling body. If he was not calm, he told himself he might leave the States without anything to show for it. With tears of defeat in his eyes, Amit stared at him. "Where are the papers?" he tried to blink the tears out of his eyes.

Jayesh Patel stared at him surprised; he had not expected it to be this easy. He waited to make sure he was serious, then he passed on a sheaf of papers for Amit to sign.

With hands shaking, Amit signed the documents, a hard ball lodged in his throat. Everything he had worked for in the past three years, it had been reduced to nothing. "It's the right choice you are making Amit," Patel said with a satisfied smile. "You would at least walk out of this with some money to your name." Amit did not bother to reply to that.

Things moved fast from there, he was allowed to make one phone call to his family and told them what was going on. His mother broke down crying when she heard the news and Amit's heart broke all over again. This was the second time he had made his mother cry since he came here eight years ago. Maybe it was for the best, he thought. He was tired of fighting where the odds were constantly against him. Home could be the reprieve he had been looking for.

The next day, Amit was put on a flight at Dulles International Airport on his way to Mumbai. He did not ignore the significance of the moment; he was being sent home from the exact same point he had been welcomed into this country. He slept throughout the flight, maybe hoping he would not have to face his reality if he was not consciously in it. When he got to the Mumbai Airport, he was not surprised to see no one was waiting for him here. He had not expected them to come anyway. He boarded a cab to his father's home. The cab driver was a very friendly smallish man, his energy could have been contagious enough for Amit to join in the conversation if he was in the mood. He tried to be polite but tried not to encourage the discussion.

Mumbai had not changed much in the eight years of his absence, the streets were still dusty and polished at the same time, the beautiful paradox that was his city. He saw a procession on the road that stopped their cab, they were all in red and were beating drums as they danced in the streets. Amit had almost forgotten what it was like to celebrate an Indian festival; the pomp, the fair and the dizzying excitement. "What are they celebrating?" he asked the driver softly.

The man turned and looked at Amit with a shocked expression, "You're Indian!" he exclaimed as if that explained anything. "How come you don't know the Holi Festival?" he looked spited and Amit kicked himself mentally. Of course, how could he have forgotten the Holi festival?

"I forgot." He whispered tritely as though apologizing to the cab driver for a crime. The man just shrugged. "How many years you been away?"

"Eight." He said, and the man just shrugged again and kept quiet for the remainder of their drive. Amit wanted peace and quiet in the cab, but he could not help but miss the chatter when it stopped. He hoped he had not offended the man in any way to make him stop talking. He found his chatter was calming his worked-up nerves in a strange way.

When they stopped at his house, his heart sank; the walls were collapsing with neglect and age, the cracks very evident. Some doors were hanging off its hinges and Amit wanted to wail. Why had his family not told him about the state of their house, he had been sending them some money, but he sure would have been able to do more if they had told him about the state of this place. His intestines twisted themselves in a tight knot of anxiety and his heart dropped into the pit of his stomach as he approached the main door. He knocked hesitantly, hoping the ground would swallow him up before it opened. Whichever God he had prayed to, had apparently not been listening. Because when the door opened, he was still there, staring into the aged face of his mother.

He watched as the recognition and shock crept into her eyes and heard her gasp of surprise as she clutched her chest. "Beta?" she whispered, not sure she could believe her eyes.

"Haa Ma," he replied reverting back to his native Hindi language seamlessly as if all those years had not been lost. At least there was a part of who he used to be that was still here somewhere. She pulled him into her arms as they cried together. She had lost a lot of weight, he could feel it. She quaked in his arms as she cried clinging onto him. Amit was not quite sure why she was crying; was it joy at seeing him or the shame and sorrow he had brought their family by coming back the way he did.

"Amit?" he turned to see his grand mom standing a little way off, peering at him through the glasses she was wearing. He went to her and touched her feet, "Yes grandma, it's me." He said his throat heavy with barely controlled tears. He touched her feet and she pulled him up into her arms while she kept whispering "Hail Lord Shiva, Hail Lord Shiva" repeatedly.

"Where is Pooja?" he asked, his voice trembling.

"She went to Kolkata for Priyanka's wedding." His mother told him sounding sad. Amit remembered her, she had been Pooja's best friend and she had had a crush on Amit for very long. He nodded and was on his way to his old room when he stopped in his tracks, his father's picture had been enlarged and put on a shrine close to the dining room. The garlands were fresh, and the candles were still smoking. Amit clasped his hands together in front of the picture before walking away hurriedly, ignoring the looks his grandmother and mother were giving him. To his eternal shame, he would not admit that he could not look at his father's eyes in the picture because he had failed the man.

When Pooja did come home, Amit was in the backyard trying to fix the back fence. He was lost in the motions of the monotonous labor when the taxi dropped them. She stopped in her tracks as she stared at him like he was a long-forgotten memory that had just resurfaced rather unpleasantly. It was her husband Abhi that approached him -as he stood motionless staring at her- to break the awkward silence and introduce himself.

"Hello brother, you must be Amit, I'm Abhi." He clasped his hands before his face in a gesture of respect to Amit. Then he carried up his little one-year old son, so Amit could see him, "Your first nephew *bhaiya*, Vikram Khanna Singh."

Amit looked down at the boy being presented to him and it felt like another punch in the gut. He looked exactly like Amit's father with his large brown eyes and button nose. The little boy was chewing on his thumb shyly, avoiding eye contact. When Amit stretched forth his hands to him, the boy accepted the hug reluctantly and then clung to Amit with a death grip, refusing to let go. Pooja came bounding towards him then, the tears flowing freely down her beautiful face. She collided into him in a hug that included her son.

"I'm sorry," he whispered in her ear as he pulled back. His eyes were waiting for and dreading the recrimination that would surely come from her. But she just shook her head and hugged him again. "I'm happy you are home brother."

****

The next few months went by fast, Amit spent most of it indoors; too ashamed to come out much. When he did manage to go out for a stroll, he could not miss the talking behind his back and the blatant mockery in the voice of the neighbors.

"I heard he stole money over there and he cheated a Patel guy in business."

"He should be ashamed of himself for showing his face here."

"He was even too busy being pretending to be American to come back for his father's funeral."

"I heard his father died of a broken heart because of him, poor Mr. Khanna."

Amit had to endure all the snide comments, he would clench his fists tight and walk away before he got too angry and told them off. Because then they would think there was truth in all their rumors and the rumors would still not die. There was one time he almost lost his cool; his cousin Sushant, the family black sheep had come back from another failed get rich quick scheme he had been chasing and finding no one else to needle for his misfortune, he came to bother Amit. In fact, he decided to make Amit's life a living hell.

"Oh look, it's the American!" he would exclaim as if excited, "Where did you stash all the money you stole? Maybe you could lend me some, some of us want to do legitimate business that would not bring shame to the family." He trailed after Amit in a drunken frenzy, jabbing at him with his fingers but Amit ignored him and kept moving. When he tried to push into Amit's room, still being loud and obnoxious, their grandma cautioned him to stop. "Leave him alone Sushant, at least he had the decency to come back with a little dignity."

"Why I am not surprised Ma, you always take his side. He is your golden boy no matter what he does."

A few days later, Abhi needed some help in moving the machinery from one building to another and Amit came out to help them. Sushant thought it would be a good opportunity to humiliate Amit again, so he started the taunts. When Amit did not reply nor reacted, he pushed him down with a satisfied smile hoping for a reaction then. A red haze covered Amit's vision and he was up from the ground in a second and had a pruning dagger to Sushant's throat before he could blink. Amit's eyes spat fire and he was satisfied to see an answering fear in Sushant's face.

"Leave me the hell alone Sushant, or else I would kill you. Do not think I haven't done it before." Before Amit could put the knife away, he felt a splattering of wetness at his feet. He looked down to find that Sushant had wet his pants and it was already trickling down to his feet. With a laugh of disgust, he pulled the knife and pushed the man away while the laborers laughed.

Amit disappeared more into his shell since then, only coming out of his room on very rare occasions. He never let anyone in; the only person he ever talked to was Vibram, Pooja's son who after getting over his initial shyness around Amit was found to be a little chatterbox. He would come back every day from kindergarten running to Amit's room on his tiny chubby legs shouting, "Amit uncle!"

Everyone else was as good as invisible to him, his room became his sanctuary, and he even avoided the family shrine and never came out for prayers or family rituals. His mother had taken it upon herself to chase away the evil eye that was upon her son and performed some rites before Amit's firmly closed doors, but still nothing happened. She was worried that he will go into state of depression and either become a loaner or lunatic if this continues. Also, Amit was the family's only bread winner after his father's death.

One day, his granny came into his room without knocking on the rare occasion when the door was open and sat at the foot of his bed, he wanted to protest but she gave him a stern look. "You will listen to all I have to say and after that we won't bother you ever again." She pointed her gnarled hands at him threateningly and continued. "Your father would have been proud of you *Beta*, I know it would be hard to believe, but you went against the odds and came back after having tried very hard. You don't need to avoid looking at your father's pictures, he is not judging you." He let his head sink onto his chest, not looking up as she continued to talk again.

"*Beta,*" she pulled his hands into her lap, "you're not a quitter or a loser. You cannot stop trying just because you encountered some hitches. It is only then your father's spirit would be sad on your behalf. Rise up son, maybe what you have always wanted is right here, but you were looking all over the World for it."

"What if I fail again Ma, I could not take it." He asked all the insecurity he felt showing on his face.

"Then you keep trying Beta, I did not raise a coward." She challenged him with her fierce dark eyes. When she finished, his shoulders were shaking with silent sobs. She gathered him into her frail arms and let him cry as she rocked him. She patted his shoulders when his sobs had reduced and left.

"Think about what I said *Beta,*" she said peering into his face before she left. One week later, she died in her sleep.

CHAPTER 14 - VICTORY AT LAST

The crushing grief that tried to overwhelm Amit was pulling him down. He tried his best to be strong, but he found he could not hold himself up, let alone his family. He knew she was old enough and her death had been painless, but he could not help the feeling of grief and the loss he felt. She had been his strength at many times when he could not find the will to go on. He had been trying for the past few days to follow her advice and find out what it was he wanted to do with his life back here. He was beginning to find the will to live again, a purpose and now she was gone.

Her funeral was a short affair, her first son; Rahul's father and in a few days, the celebrations and rites were all done. Amit decided then that her death was going to be the turning point in his life; he had the option to sink deeper into his pit of defeat or climb out and make something out of his life. So, he chose the latter option.

Amit was looking into applying to some tech companies in Mumbai, but nothing worked out. He sent in resumes to many companies outside of Mumbai but still there was no luck whatsoever for him. Most of the good I.T jobs were in Bangalore or Hyderabad and he did not want to leave his mother on her own especially after granny's death. Also, his skills (had become rusty) were more of a game developer and the game industry was gradually expanding in India. Market was controlled by 10-12 companies which made games for PCs or phones. Most of the games were either car race, cricket, casino or shooting games.

He was about to get discouraged when something came through for him in a very unlikely form. He came home from a job hunt, tired and frustrated. He was about to go to sleep when he stumbled on a notebook he had unpacked while he was looking for something to wear. It was the notebook where he had kept scores and notes on a game prototype he had been working with when he was in G-DUB. He had gotten his roommates, Manoj and Brian to test the game he had been working on then. He had forgotten all of that in the midst of the craziness of September 11th and school work and being a teaching assistant.

He studied the notes and went on his laptop, realizing he was seeing an angle he had not noticed before testing the prototype. He ransacked his bag, hoping that prototype was among the few belongings he had left United States with. His search was fruitful, and they were still there. He started working through the app and its modifications and before he knew it, it was morning and he had not slept a wink. Actually, the game was ahead of its time and used artificial intelligence and virtual reality to solve World problems. The game had a list of historical events such as Indian independence, U.S.S.R split, Palestine-Israel crisis and the players could select the event and then used their strategy to avert the crisis. Virtual reality headphones gave the players the ability to be present in that time. It was almost like being part of "Back to the Future" movie.

The game had a data piece where historical information was gathered from internet and the plot kept changing as new strategies were suggested by players. The game was addictive since people were interested in solving historical World problems and learning about history by being there first hand (in a virtual environment). It was also a good way to experience different eras. There was the education aspect of this which could have resonated with educational institutions and museums. Amit was super excited about this for once he had found something he loved and wanted to do as much as he loved running a restaurant. His goal was to save money to use as a down payment to borrow more money for VR equipment and hire other developers. The game required internet connection since it was getting historical information from Wikipedia (Wikipedia had an Application process interface). Unfortunately, in India the internet speed was still not that fast and the games were hardly pulling any data from the internet. Although Amit was confident of the game and its stickiness, there were some concerns about the internet speed and whether he will be able to find the right company to market his game. However his motivation to do something big (to prove it to the World) overpowered his fears and inhibitions. In most of his dreams he was falling off of a sky scrapper being rescued by Granny or drowning in an ocean being rescued by his Dad.

Video game development is a pretty labor-intensive process. The effort is undertaken by a game developer, who may range from a single person to an international team dispersed across the globe. Traditional commercial PC and console games are normally funded by a publisher and can take several years to reach completion. Indie games can take less time and can be produced at a lower cost by individuals and smaller developers. The independent game industry has seen a substantial rise in recent years with the growth of new online distribution systems, such as Steam and Uplay, as well as the mobile game market, such as for Android and iOS devices.

The first video games were non-commercial, and were developed in the 1960s. They required mainframe computers to run and were not available to the general public. Commercial game development began in the 1970s with the advent of first-generation video game consoles and early home computers like the Apple I. Due to low costs and low capabilities of computers, a lone programmer could develop a full game. However, approaching the 21st century, ever-increasing computer processing power and heightened consumer expectations made it difficult for a single person to produce a mainstream console or PC game. The average cost of producing a triple-A video game slowly rose from US$1–4 million in 2000 to over $5 million in 2006, then to over $20 million by 2010.

Mainstream PC and console games were generally developed in phases. First, in pre-production, pitches, prototypes, and game design documents were written. If the idea was approved and the developer received funding, a full-scale development began. This usually involved a team of 20–100 individuals with various responsibilities, including designers, artists, programmers, and testers.

A game developer could be a single individual to a large multinational company. There were both independent and publisher-owned studios. Independent developers relied on financial support from a game publisher. They usually had to develop a game from concept to prototype without external funding. The formal game proposal was then submitted to publishers, who financed the game development from several months to years. The publisher would retain exclusive rights to distribute and market the game and would often own the intellectual property rights for the game franchise. Publisher's company also owned the developer's company in some cases and generally the publisher was the one who owned the game's intellectual property rights.

He had used the money from his savings, renovating his family house and upgrading the home appliances.

His first big break came when John Abraham gave him a call.

He was in his room trying to get some sleep after staying up all night working on the game when his phone rang, "Hello, can I speak to Mr. Khanna.?" Amit rolled his eyes thinking it was one of these fake American companies that resided in India.

"Yes, this is him." He answered in a bored monotone.

"This is John Abraham." Amit sat upright in a bolt, his boredom disappearing from his tone.

"The John Abraham?" he asked disbelievingly.

The voice on the other end laughed heartily before answering; "Yes, the same one."

"Uhmmm, it's a pleasure to meet you sir. How did you get my number?" his voice was flustered, and he could not help the stammering. John Abraham was a Bollywood actor and his hit movie Race 2 was already trending on the charts. How was John Abraham calling him?

"I own a gaming company and I saw the prototype you put online for your game. I'm willing to make an offer for it. Would you come to the office, so we could discuss this?"

"Yes…. Uhmm yes sir!" Amit stared at the phone when the man hung up not believing his ears. John Abraham! John Abraham wanted to buy his game!! He pinched himself, so he would be sure this was not a dream, but it still felt surreal. He had not expected anything from the game, he had just been working on it, so he would have something to do to relax when he was not programming. He had heard of the gaming company Top Game and Co. They were one of the best in India and he was honored they even considered him.

The scheduled day of the meeting, Amit dressed up in his best suit, a souvenir from his momentary days of fortune in Washington DC when business was very good. He had splurged on an expensive tuxedo that now proved to be handy. His mom gave him the Prasad in his hands and gave him a big hug.

"Why don't you stay positive *Beta?* You never know what you would find today." She was as excited even more so than him which was understandable because she was a huge fan of John Abrahams. He had endured her telling him all the promptings she had given him to make sure that he mentioned her to the man.

TopGame and Co. was a big company Amit thought as he stared up at the impressive edifice that was the company. The inside was as impressive as the outside too. The décor was a mixture of bright white and a cool blue. The receptionist directed him to a waiting room where he could wait for Mr. Abraham. Before long, the man was there, and Amit was impressed by his ability to keep to time which was a hard thing to obtain amongst successful businessmen these days.

"Mr. Khanna, right?" the man came forward amidst the people milling around him and following him everywhere. He approached Amit and shook his hand firmly with a warm smile. "Please, follow me." He gestured to an office a little down the hall, it was in fact a conference room and there were about twelve people in the room.

"This is my team, they also sit on the board, so we would like to make a pitch." The man's enthusiasm and energy seemed to draw people like a magnet to himself. He gestured to Amit to sit and they made their offer. 200 million dollars. Amit was shocked and floored by the offer, he had not come out today sure he wanted to sell, but after all the negotiations and considerations, they settled for 250 million dollars and a retained ownership of the game software plus the agreement to update and upgrade the software anytime it was required. And just like that, Amit Khanna was rich!

Things moved on so fast from there, there were agreements to sign, people to meet and the game launch. He was given a team of designers, developers and testers to work with. The launch date was set and all the hard work was finally paying off. He also became the brand ambassador for TopGames and Co. and designed other games for the company. In just short of two years since he came back, he was a household name.

As a move to give back to society, Amit built a school and named it after his father. "The Suraj Khanna Memorial Institute of Learning". The school was inaugurated by his mother and all the dignitaries were present for the inauguration including the Prime Minister. "How can we keep our students here, Amit?" asked the PM. Amit was a little surprised by the question but responded promptly. "Let's make their dreams come true at home. "PM invited him to Delhi to help him out in his initiative. A Trust fund was created with the help of the Indian Prime Minister to help the youth of India. Government was ready to sponsor the higher education of students as long as they came back from foreign countries and helped Indian Government in implementing new ideas in different sectors. Amit went from city to city, promoting this initiative.

On one of the trips, he bumped into someone at the Delhi airport lobby. Literally he bumped into her, with her luggage and sent it all flying away.

"Oh, I'm sorry she said, without looking up as she packed up her luggage. "Forgive my clumsiness." She must have sensed his shock and silence because she looked up then. "Amit?" she said in a shocked whisper, not believing her eyes.

"Lisa, what on earth are you doing in India?" he tried to mask his shock with a frown.

"I have just moved here for a job position at the college of engineering in Delhi."

"I didn't know you loved teaching." He scrutinized her face as he interrogated her.

She shrugged simply, "Sometimes we surprise ourselves Amit."

She could not have been more right with that observation. He looked her over hating the way his heart still beat out of rhythm at the sight of her. Apparently, he was a one-woman man, seeing as he found it very hard to get over one woman who had gotten under his skin. He looked at her fingers and they were curiously bare. "Uhmm, so you're not married?"

"Divorced." She gave a bashful smile. "What about you, Amit?"

"Still single." She nodded and turned to leave. "I guess I'll keep going then, see you around Amit."

"Wait!" Amit panicked, hoping he was not going to blow this. "Can I see you again sometime?"

Her smile was wide and pure and beautiful just as Amit had remembered. "Yes, I would love that." She gave him her address at the college and took his card then with a spring in her steps, she left.

Amit smiled to himself as he walked away. He really had been blessed back here. He was doing the humanitarian work he loved, he was successful in every sense of the word and he had the only woman he had ever loved back in his life. Yes, it had not come in the package he had wanted, but he had kept his heart open and found it.